Miranda took the first deep breath her lungs would allow during the last hour.

The exact amount of time Andrew Noble had been in the restaurant.

An ember of disgust flared inside her. People struggled to make ends meet while men like Andrew Noble spent money they hadn't even worked for. A poster boy for the idle rich.

An incredibly good-looking poster boy...

Miranda tried to shake the thought away before it took hold and formed an image of perfectly chiseled features, tousled black hair and eyes a warm palette of soft greens and browns.

Too late.

* * *

A Tiny Blessings Tale: Loving families and needy children continue to come together to fulfill God's greatest plans!

FOR HER SON'S LOVE
Kathryn Springer (LI #404) July 2007

MISSIONARY DADDY
Linda Goodnight (LI #408) August 2007

A MOMMY IN MIND
Arlene James (LI #412) September 2007

LITTLE MISS MATCHMAKER
Dana Corbit (LI #416) October 2007

GIVING THANKS FOR BABY
Terri Reed (LI #420) November 2007

A HOLIDAY TO REMEMBER
Jillian Hart (LI #424) December 2007

Books by Kathryn Springer

Love Inspired

Tested by Fire #266
Her Christmas Wish #324
By Her Side #360
For Her Son's Love #404

Steeple Hill Single Title

Front Porch Princess

KATHRYN SPRINGER

is a lifelong resident of Wisconsin. Growing up in a newspaper family, she spent long hours as a child plunking out stories on her mother's typewriter. She wrote her first "book" at the age of ten and hasn't stopped writing since then! Kathryn began writing inspirational romance because it allows her to combine her faith in God with her love of a happy ending.

For Her Son's Love

Kathryn Springer

Published by Steeple Hill Books™

Special thanks and acknowledgment are given to Kathryn Springer for her contribution to A TINY BLESSINGS TALE miniseries.

STEEPLE HILL BOOKS

ISBN-13: 978-0-373-87440-8
ISBN-10: 0-373-87440-5

FOR HER SON'S LOVE

This edition published by arrangement with Steeple Hill Books.

www.SteepleHill.com

Printed in U.S.A.

"See, I have engraved you on the palms of my hands."

—*Isaiah* 49:16

To Char—Just because

Chapter One

The last time Andrew Noble visited Chestnut Grove had been eight months ago, when he'd shown up to surprise his cousin, Rachel, on her birthday. This time, it was to fire her.

He hoped the bouquet of peach roses tucked in the crook of his arm would soften the blow.

Andrew bypassed the spacious reception area of the Noble Foundation and veered toward the stairs that led to the suite of offices on the top floor of the building. Rachel didn't know he was in town and Andrew didn't want anyone to warn her. For what he had to do, keeping the element of surprise might be in his favor. He hoped she'd be so happy to see him—and the bouquet of her favorite flowers—that she'd cheerfully hand over the Foundation's checkbook.

Right.

Even though they had practically grown up together and were more like siblings than first cousins, the Noble

Foundation was Rachel's baby. Her parents, Beatrice and Charles, may have founded the organization, which raised money for worthwhile charities, but Rachel's energy, drive and creativity had pushed its reputation and influence beyond the boundaries of Virginia. At the moment, her commitment wasn't in question; her energy level was.

It was the reason his mother, at the urging of his aunt Beatrice, had tracked him down at a friend's beach house in Malibu the day before.

Andrew wasn't sure if he should be flattered or insulted that his name had been the one pulled out of the family hat.

Rachel was expecting a baby at the end of the summer and according to Eli Cavanaugh, Rachel's husband, she'd been feeling unusually fatigued over the past few weeks. Eli had finally gotten her to admit she'd experienced some bouts of dizziness, too. Even though pediatrics, not obstetrics, was Eli's specialty, he'd shared his concern with Beatrice, who'd shared it with Andrew's mother. They'd decided someone needed to step in and temporarily ease the reins of the Foundation out of Rachel's capable hands.

That someone was him. Apparently, the old adage "desperate times call for desperate measures" held some truth.

Andrew exhaled in relief when he saw there was no one at the desk that guarded the entrance to Rachel's corner office. The staff had a tendency to protect Rachel as if she were the Hope diamond.

He pushed open the door, expecting to see his

prototype-for-the-Type-A-personality cousin hard at work. What he saw instead made his blood run cold—Rachel sound asleep in the leather chair, her bare feet propped up on the desk. At nine o'clock in the morning.

He coughed lightly.

Rachel's body jerked and she bolted upright, wide awake.

"Andrew!"

With a cry of delight, Rachel pushed herself out of the chair and waddled into his arms. "What are you doing here? The baby isn't due for another few months. Or are you planning to pull another one of your famous disappearing acts on us again?"

Andrew planted a kiss on her cheek, not missing the purple shadows under her eyes and the lines of fatigue bracketing her mouth. Guilt kicked in as he realized his aunt hadn't exaggerated Rachel's condition. He didn't know anything about pregnant women, but even to his inexperienced eyes she looked completely worn out.

He decided honesty was the best policy.

"I'm here to take over the Noble Foundation. By force, if necessary, but I'm hoping these roses will do the trick."

Rachel accepted the bouquet, her expression wry. "You heard."

Andrew sauntered over to the leather chair and sat down. "Word on the street is that you haven't been feeling well."

"I should have known. Our mothers are ganging up on me and they sent *you* to do their dirty work." Rachel crossed her arms over her bulging abdomen. "It's just normal pregnancy stuff. I *am* carrying the equivalent of an airline-approved carry-on around my middle."

Andrew just looked at her until she gave an irritated little huff. "You can lower that arrogant eyebrow of yours. I admit it. Dr. Bingham is a little concerned about the swelling in my hands and feet. Overly concerned, if you ask me. He and Eli are friends, so…" Her eyes narrowed. "Did *Eli* call you?"

"I plead the Fifth." Andrew grinned. "I received an order from the top to take control of things here while you go home, put your feet up and watch the cooking channel."

Rachel scowled.

"Or knit baby booties."

The flash of longing in her eyes surprised him. "I don't knit."

"You don't cook, either, but that hasn't stopped you from trying to master it. For the past two years."

"Did I ever tell you that you're my favorite cousin? Because if I did, I take it back. And all the other nice things I might have said to inflate your already enormous ego—"

The intercom interrupted her. Rachel reached for the phone but Andrew beat her to it. "What's your secretary's name?"

"Zoe." Rachel tried to pluck the phone out of his hand.

"Andrew Noble." He winced as a high-pitched squeak pinched his eardrum. Probably because he'd managed to sneak in when she'd abandoned her post. "What can I do for you, Zoe?"

Rachel attempted another hostile takeover so Andrew swiveled the chair around. "Tell Mr. Chrone I'll be the one meeting with him tomorrow morning about the estate. That's right. Me." Andrew hung up the phone and faced his cousin again. "Why are you still here?"

"What did they bribe you with to come to Chestnut Grove?" Rachel demanded. "Virginia is a long way from Rhode Island. Whatever it was, I'll double it if you leave quietly."

"No one bribed me." Andrew shrugged. "I'm the only one in the family who leads the kind of wastrel existence that allows me to take over a huge charitable organization without advanced notice. Not that I'm not qualified to spend other people's money. I've been doing that with Great-Grandpa's trust fund for years."

The flicker of sadness in Rachel's eyes scraped against Andrew's conscience. She might not listen to the gossip but she read the papers. There was no getting around the fact that, over the years, his reputation as an irresponsible playboy had stained the fabric of the Noble family. Still, they'd remained stubbornly loyal to him. Especially Rachel.

Sending up a prayer for forgiveness, he used that loyalty to his advantage. "Unless you don't trust me?"

She rolled her eyes. "Please. Your smile will probably raise more money in a day than I could in a month. It's just that...there's no reason for all this fuss. I'm fine."

Andrew might have believed her if she hadn't ended the sentence by yawning.

"You don't have to prove anything, Rachel. Let me take care of the Foundation while you take care of yourself and the baby. If Bingham gives you the green light to keep working, I'll abdicate the throne." He patted the leather armrests on the chair. "I promise."

Because he expected round two, the sudden relief in her eyes stunned him.

"Fine. You win. You can even move into my loft if you need a place to stay. And come for dinner—"

Andrew had tasted Rachel's cooking, and she was more gifted in the boardroom than she was the kitchen. "The Starlight Diner is just down the street."

He laughed when Rachel glowered at him.

"If you need anything—"

"I'll ask Zoe."

"Mr. Chrone—"

"Collects baseball cards and raises African Violets," Andrew finished.

"All right." She didn't move.

Andrew arched a brow. "Now what do you need?"

She grinned and wiggled her bare toes in the carpet. "My shoes. They're under the desk."

"Billionaire bachelor alert." Miranda Jones looked up as Darcy, the young waitress who shared the breakfast and lunch shift with her at the Starlight Diner, swept into the kitchen and gave her a teasing grin. "And he's sitting in *your* section. Again."

Andrew Noble.

Miranda's concentration dissolved. If a list of the world's most eligible bachelors existed, Andrew's name probably appeared at the top of it. The Noble family was the equivalent of American royalty and Andrew, the prince. The media loved him, even if all they could report were the details of his latest adventure in some exotic locale or the name of the woman who happened to be at his side for one of the Noble Foundation's many fund-raising events.

He'd come into the diner earlier in the week and Miranda guessed he was visiting his cousin, Rachel Cavanaugh. Why he'd chosen the Starlight instead of one of Richmond's swanky, award-winning restaurants, she had no idea. And now he was back. Three days later.

"You can wait on him," she murmured. "I have to deliver this order to the boys at table five before they waste away."

Darcy's gum snapped in surprise, but then she grinned. "I'm not going to turn down *that* tip. Or the chance to stare into those dreamy eyes." She sighed dramatically and put one hand over her heart.

"What about Greg?" Miranda felt compelled to bring up the name of the young deliveryman Darcy had been mooning over for the last two weeks.

"Greg? Greg who?" Darcy winked and straightened the collar of her pink polo shirt—the standard uniform of the diner waitstaff. She sashayed out of the kitchen, humming "Someday My Prince Will Come" under her breath.

Miranda exhaled in relief. Maybe she had just given up a generous tip but something about Andrew Noble flustered her.

You mean, other than the obvious, a voice in her head mocked. *That he's incredibly easy on the eyes and wealthy enough to live a life of leisure?*

Something a working girl like her couldn't begin to

fathom. She'd never had a problem dealing with a customer before but, when Andrew had walked into the diner, her heart had responded with an unsettling kick. Darcy would welcome his attention. Miranda wished he'd find another restaurant.

"M.J. Snap out of it! Order up!" Isaac Tubman's exasperated shout echoed around the kitchen. And probably the entire dining room. But no one would blink an eye. The regulars were used to the gruff old cook and his occasional tirades.

"Sorry." Miranda scooped up the tray of hamburgers and took a step toward the swinging doors that separated the kitchen from the dining area.

"Don't forget the garnish!" Isaac thundered, stopping her in her tracks.

"You've been watching Emeril again, haven't you?" Miranda smiled but dutifully dropped a sprig of wilted parsley onto each plate.

Miranda heard Isaac chuckle as he turned back to the grill. She'd worked at the diner for four years, both as a waitress and a bookkeeper, and she'd learned right away that Isaac's bark was worse than his bite. When her son, Daniel, had developed bronchitis shortly after Sandra Lange had hired her, it was Isaac who'd shown up at their apartment one evening with a container of homemade chicken noodle soup and his wooden checkerboard to entertain the little boy, giving her a much needed break.

In spite of Miranda's reluctance to accept help from anyone, the simple gesture had endeared her to the old cook. As a single parent, Miranda had gotten used to doing everything on her own, But Daniel, her thoughtful, wise-beyond-his-years son, had taken to Isaac immediately.

Two years later, Isaac still kept the checkerboard behind the soda fountain for the times Miranda had to bring Daniel to work with her.

Balancing the tray in her hands, Miranda pushed through the doors, no longer feeling as if she were passing through a time warp when she stepped out of the modern kitchen into the 1950s-style dining area. "Rock Around the Clock" blared out of the juke box, not quite drowning out the cheer from the teenage boys who saw her approaching with their burgers.

The commotion snagged Andrew Noble's attention. He glanced up and their eyes met.

The pictures of him that frequently graced the society page of the *Richmond Gazette* didn't do him justice. Black ink might have accurately captured the color of his hair, but it didn't give a hint that his eyes were a warm, sunlight-in-the-woods shade of hazel. The lazy half smile he directed at the cameras—the one that gave him an air of mystery and drove the gossip columnists crazy—was even more potent in real life.

She could attest to that because at the moment it was directed right at her.

Miranda quickly averted her eyes and broke the connection.

She refused to act like a starstruck groupie. Men like Andrew Noble wielded too much power. And she knew from bitter experience that men could use their position and power to hurt other people. Hal had taught her that lesson and she wasn't going to let history repeat itself. Not when the wounds he'd inflicted had yet to heal.

At table five, eager hands reached for the tray. They reminded Miranda of Daniel and she smiled. "Patience, boys. The burgers aren't going to walk off the plates."

She divvied up the order and went to the soda fountain to refill their drinks. The boys came in every Friday for lunch and Miranda knew them by name. She also knew the grand sum of her tip would be the handful of change they pooled in the center of the table before they left. They meant well, although a dollar tip wasn't going to have a significant impact on her meager savings account. Over the past few months, Daniel had sprouted like Jack's beanstalk, outgrowing all his clothes from the previous summer. Which meant a trip to the mall in Richmond was needed.

Miranda tried to suppress the wave of discouragement that threatened to crash over her. She'd find a way. Sandra was always willing to let her pick up another shift if she needed it.

"Andrew!" As if conjured up by Miranda's thoughts, Sandra's lilting voice swept through the diner. She made a habit of chatting with each and every customer who came into the Starlight.

Sandra gave Miranda's arm an affectionate pat as she breezed past and paused to talk to Andrew. "It's nice to see you again. I figured you'd be long gone by now."

"I'm afraid Chestnut Grove is stuck with me for a while." Andrew's New England accent was clipped but pleasant, and Miranda resisted the urge to look at him again, to see if the smile she heard in his voice was reflected in his eyes. "Rachel's been feeling a little tired lately so I'm going to keep an eye on things at the Foundation."

Which meant he wasn't just passing through town. Miranda felt a strange mixture of relief and dread bubble up inside of her. It was the relief that disturbed her.

"Rachel and the baby are all right, aren't they?" The concern in Sandra's voice stilled Miranda's hands as she waited to hear Andrew's response. Rachel and her friends had been coming to the Starlight for brunch every Sunday after church for as long as she'd worked at the diner.

"She has an appointment with her doctor this morning, which will give us a better indication about what's going on."

"Please tell Rachel I'll add her and Eli and the baby to my prayer list," Sandra said.

"She'll appreciate that, Ms. Lange."

"Sandra," she said, correcting him. "This is the Starlight Diner, my dear, not the Ritz."

"I'll remember that, Sandra."

The warmth in his voice somehow made him seem more approachable. Miranda could almost imagine he was just another one of the diner's regulars.

In Armani.

"Sandra! Order up!" Isaac's voice boomed above the music and the steady hum of conversation.

"Someone should remind that man *I'm* the one who owns the place." Sandra laughed and maneuvered her way back through the maze of tables, greeting people by name on her way to the kitchen.

Miranda double-checked the bill before she presented it to the boys and then turned to slip away.

Andrew Noble was looking right at her. Again.

Miranda couldn't blame the jolt that coursed through her on Isaac's high-octane coffee. She'd only had one cup since her shift had started.

"I'd like a refill when you have a minute—" his eyes drifted to her name tag "—Miranda."

She nodded but it didn't feel like a *normal* nod. It felt like she'd suddenly turned into one of those bobble-headed dolls. "I'll tell Darcy."

Where was Darcy?

Feeling slightly panicked, Miranda scanned the diner but there was no sign of the girl anywhere.

"I think she's busy with a cleanup on aisle six," Andrew said helpfully.

Miranda lowered her gaze and sure enough, Darcy was crouched next to a portable high chair, mopping up a waterfall of fruit punch cascading over the side of the tray.

So much for avoiding Andrew Noble.

Chapter Two

Miranda.

Andrew watched her stop and chat briefly with an elderly gentleman who sat alone at a table. She was smiling again but it wasn't the distant, polite one she'd bestowed upon him. No. This one was natural. It momentarily transformed her entire face, softening the curve of her lips and bringing a faint blush of color to her cheeks.

He'd noticed her the first time he'd come into the diner a few days ago. And he wasn't sure why. With her hair secured in a severe twist at the nape of her neck and not a speck of makeup on her face, she obviously wasn't the kind of woman who tried to court attention.

In fact, it seemed as if she'd gone out of her way to avoid him.

And she was doing it again.

Which—he hated to admit—chipped at his pride a little. He wasn't used to women running in the opposite direction when they saw him.

For crying out loud. Get over yourself, Noble.

"Excuse me." She returned with the coffeepot and Andrew pushed his cup closer. He tried to make eye contact but she didn't cooperate, intent on searching for something in the pocket of her apron rather than looking at him.

"Cream or sugar?" She finally glanced up, long enough for him to glimpse captivating flecks of gold in her autumn-brown eyes.

"Cream. Thank you." It was all he could come up with. Andrew wanted to bang his head against the table. He'd had dinner with heads of state and vacationed with celebrities, but a slender waitress with soulful eyes had suddenly reduced his vocabulary to that of a three-year-old. A very shy three-year-old.

"M.J.!" Isaac poked his head out of the pass-through between the kitchen and dining room. "Where are you? The cheese on this burger is aging. I'm going to have to raise the price if it sits up here any longer."

Andrew saw Miranda bite her lip to hold back a laugh and took advantage of the moment to draw her out. "What does the *J* stand for?"

Wariness instantly replaced the laughter that backlit her eyes. "Jones."

Andrew got the impression that only the Starlight's reputation as a friendly diner prevented her from ignoring his question.

He opened his mouth to say something—anything—else but she beat him to it. "If you need something, just get Darcy's attention."

On cue, the young woman who'd been sidetracked

by the toddler's spill dashed over to his table. Her eyes sparkled and her smile bordered on flirtatious. If her bleach-blond hair hadn't been pulled back in a ponytail, Andrew was sure she would have given it one of those teasing, off-the-shoulder flips.

"Are you interested in dessert today, Mr. Noble?"

Andrew buried a sigh. *That* was what he was used to.

"Not today. The boss only gives me an hour for lunch."

She giggled. "Me, too!" Her tone clearly implied that now they had something in common. Andrew looked for Miranda but she'd disappeared into the kitchen.

Fortunately, Sandra came to his rescue.

"Darcy!" She motioned the waitress over to the counter.

The waitress's shoulders drooped but she gave Andrew an irrepressible smile. "If you need a warm-up—on your coffee, just holler."

In spite of his overzealous waitress, Andrew lingered at the diner until the lunch crowd cleared out. Maybe it was because there wasn't a single thing on the menu preceded by the words *light* or *fat-free.* Or because Isaac and Sandra treated him the way they did everyone else who came through the door—with down-home charm and a complete lack of pretense.

Or maybe it's because you're hoping to get another glimpse of Miranda Jones.

What was it about her that piqued his interest? She was pretty in an understated way, but something else about her intrigued him.

Because she didn't write her phone number on your bill?

That brought back an unwelcome memory. A few years ago, one of the newspapers had taken his picture while he'd toured a coast guard cutter. A photographer had caught him off guard, capturing the bored expression on his face. It was a direct contrast to the adoring gaze of the officer's daughter who'd latched on to his arm like a barnacle on the hull of the ship at the beginning of the tour. The tongue-in-cheek caption accompanying the photo had humorously noted that Andrew seemed to be more interested in the *search* than the *rescue.*

Andrew had developed a thick skin over the years when it came to the outrageous claims the gossip columns printed, but that one still bothered him. Especially because he wondered if there wasn't some truth to it.

He did lose interest. Quickly.

Which made him a little afraid that he was *that* guy. The guy who couldn't commit. Or maybe it was because he'd never met a woman who was more interested in his life than his *lifestyle.*

The cell phone suddenly vibrated in his pocket. He would have ignored it if Rachel's name wasn't the one displayed on the tiny screen. They'd grown up together and, because they were only a few years apart in age, they seemed more like siblings than cousins. Which meant he couldn't pass up an opportunity to tease her when he answered the phone.

"This is Andrew Noble, temporary administrator of the Noble Foundation."

"Not so temporary, I'm afraid."

Andrew's smile faded at the discouragement in Rachel's voice. "What did Dr. Bingham say?"

"I... Here. Can you talk to Eli for a minute?" Rachel's voice cracked.

"Sure." Andrew sent up a quick, silent prayer that whatever Rachel and Eli were facing, God would give them the strength they needed to endure it.

"Andrew?" Eli's voice shook a little, too. "Dr. Bingham diagnosed Rachel with preeclampsia. And he put her on bed rest until the baby comes."

"Pre what?" Andrew tried to process the word and drew a blank.

"Preeclampsia. He said it's not uncommon for a first pregnancy and because we caught it early, she and the baby should be fine."

Should be fine.

"So what can Bingham do to cure it?" He siphoned out the concern he felt and deliberately kept his tone brisk; if there was a diagnosis, there had to be a cure. This was the twenty-first century....

"There is no cure." Eli's next words shot his theory all to pieces. "The only thing that takes care of it is delivering the baby, but it's too soon. That's why Dr. Bingham is putting Rachel on bed rest."

Rachel and bed rest.

"I know." Eli sighed, as if he'd read Andrew's mind. "We're on our way home now but Rachel wants to talk to you again."

"Andrew?" Rachel didn't sound at all like the take-charge woman he knew and loved. "I know you were coerced into running the Foundation but you had no idea it was going to be for more than a few days. I'm officially letting you off the hook. Mom and Dad can hire someone—"

"Don't worry about it. The only thing I have planned for the next few months is a trip to St. Bart's…and a race in Monaco. No one will miss me."

The clink of silverware distracted him. Andrew had been so focused on the conversation he hadn't realized someone was clearing the booth right behind him. He glanced over his shoulder just in time to see Miranda Jones walking away.

"If you're sure…" Rachel's voice faded and Andrew knew the reality of the situation was sinking in.

"All I want you to do is let Eli tuck you into bed with the remote control and your knitting needles. I'll be over this evening with a gallon of mint chocolate-chip ice cream."

"Andrew…thanks. I know St. Bart's is a lot more fun than sitting behind a desk."

"I'm praying for you," Andrew murmured. "God wasn't surprised by this—trust Him. He's going to get you through it."

He snapped the phone shut and stared out the window, knowing he had to take his own advice.

Okay, Lord, what's up? Because if You wanted to work on building patience in Rachel, couldn't You have picked something a little easier? Like a really long red light at the intersection?

He did a quick calculation. The baby wasn't due until the end of summer. This derailed his schedule in unforeseen ways. He *did* have plans to go to St. Bart's and he *was* sponsoring a new driver—but there were other commitments he couldn't share with Rachel. Or anyone else.

The feet on the Elvis Presley clock on the wall began to dance, reminding him breaktime was officially over. He had to go back to the Foundation to tell the employees the good news—that the guy who had a reputation as a spendthrift playboy was about to take over the distribution of millions of dollars to worthwhile charities.

Judging from the cautious looks he'd been getting all week, everyone expected him to mess up. And it wasn't as if he could put their minds at ease. Not without totally destroying the image he'd spent years cultivating.

Andrew passed the table a pack of teenage boys had taken over earlier and noticed the pile of change—mostly dimes and nickels—next to the ketchup bottle. That was all those kids could scrape together? They probably spent more renting a video game.

He looked around to make sure no one was watching and discreetly tucked a ten-dollar bill between the ketchup and mustard bottles, hoping it would put a smile on Miranda Jones's face.

"Bye, Andrew. You have a good afternoon now." Sandra popped up from behind the counter as he moved toward the door. "And come back soon."

When Miranda peeked out of the kitchen and saw the empty booth by the window, she took the first deep breath her lungs would allow during the last hour. The exact amount of time Andrew Noble had been in the diner.

St. Bart's. Monaco. And he'd dropped the names so matter-of-factly. As if he were going to the grocery store and then on his way home, he planned to swing by the Laundromat.

An ember of disgust flared inside her. People struggled to make ends meet while men like Andrew Noble went from one source of entertainment to another, spending money they hadn't even worked for. A poster boy for the idle rich.

An incredibly good-looking poster boy....

Miranda tried to shake the thought away before it took hold and formed an image of perfectly chiseled features, tousled black hair and eyes a warm palette of soft greens and browns.

Too late.

Okay, he was good-looking. She could admit it. So was a mile-high slice of Sandra's French silk pie. Solid proof that not everything that looked good was good for you.

And there was no point even thinking about Andrew Noble. The diner might be conveniently located down the street from the Noble Foundation but he wouldn't be back. In the world he inhabited, filet mignon was the staple, not chicken-fried steak with a side of mashed potatoes.

Darcy came alongside her, waving a crisp ten-dollar bill. "This is for you. I already cleared tables four and five. And here I thought Mr. Gorgeous and Available would be the big tipper of the day."

Miranda frowned. Table four had been Mr. Walrich, whose standing order of a piece of banana-cream pie and a cup of coffee garnered her a shiny fifty-cent piece as a tip. That left the boys at table five....

"Maybe it's back pay for all the times they didn't leave you a tip," Darcy joked.

"If that were true, I'd be able to send Daniel to Harvard," Miranda said, tucking the bill into her apron pocket. "But who am I to complain?"

"I sure wouldn't be complaining if Andrew Noble had written his phone number on the five-dollar bill he left me," Darcy said, a blissful expression on her face.

Miranda choked back a laugh, earning a pout from Darcy.

"What? It happened in the novel I just finished. I thought it was very romantic."

"Men like Andrew Noble don't work that way."

Darcy crossed her arms. "How *do* men like Andrew Noble work, oh, Wise One?"

"Maybe he has his butler call your maid. Or maybe if you dropped one of your Birkenstocks on the sidewalk out front—"

"You think?" Darcy's eyes went wide until she realized Miranda was teasing her. "Just because you don't believe in happily ever after doesn't mean you have to ruin it for the rest of us, Miranda Jones!"

She flounced away.

Miranda knew Darcy's offended tone was exaggerated but the words still stung.

She *didn't* believe in happily ever after.

Not anymore.

Andrew was lost in thought, alternately praying for Rachel, Eli and their unborn child, and wondering just how he was going to run the Foundation and keep his other…commitments.

He rounded the corner where he'd parked the car

and stumbled over something. Since the startled gasp came from somewhere near his kneecap, he knew it was a *small* something. Or rather, *someone.*

"Sorry!" A boy about seven or eight years old sat on the concrete next to a bicycle. Or, more accurately, had been taken prisoner by it. The brown towel knotted around his shoulders had snagged in the chain.

Andrew hid a smile and crouched down to help. He remembered using his mother's towels to create a similar costume when he was young. "Got into some trouble here, hmm?"

A face, almost completely swallowed up by a pair of lime-green swim goggles, peered up at him. "Yeah."

Andrew's gaze skimmed over him, assessing the damage, but, in spite of the two skinned knees, the boy sounded more disgruntled than hurt.

A teenage girl, weighted down by a colorful beach bag slung over her shoulder, sprinted up to them and knelt beside Andrew.

"Are you okay, Daniel? I don't know why you insisted on tying the towel on like that. You weren't wearing those stupid goggles, were you? Where are your glasses? Your mom's going to kill me—"

Color rushed into the boy's dirt-smudged cheeks.

"There doesn't seem to be too much damage," Andrew interrupted, stepping in to save the boy further embarrassment. He lowered his voice. "One of the hazards of *the job,* right?"

Daniel slanted a quick look at him but Andrew kept his expression serious, which earned a hesitant nod.

The girl sighed dramatically as she watched Andrew

work the corner of the towel out of the bicycle chain. “Look at that grease smear on your mom’s towel. That’s never going to come out. I’m going to the diner to get us some ice cream. And some Band-Aids. I’ll be right back. Don’t you dare move, Daniel.”

She stalked away and Andrew caught a glimpse of shame lingering in the brown eyes behind the goggles.

“Don’t be discouraged, Daniel,” he said quietly. “Not everyone gets it.”

At Daniel’s age, he’d been partial to using the roof of the garden shed as a launch pad for flying lessons. No sense giving the kid any ideas, though.

Daniel gifted him with a smile, revealing a gap where one of his front teeth should have been.

“Let’s make sure you’re good to go.” Andrew checked the chain one more time.

“Here comes Hallie. All she wants to do is talk on the phone. I think she’s one of the bad guys,” the boy confided in a whisper.

Andrew’s lips twitched. “Don’t be too hard on her—she’s just a civilian. Your mom and dad wouldn’t hire one of *them* to take care of you during the day.”

“It’s just me and Mom,” Daniel said matter-of-factly as he hopped back on his bike, pushing his feet against the concrete to propel himself forward. Probably to intercept the sitter, who marched toward them. “I gotta go.”

It’s just me and Mom.

Andrew could relate to that, too. Even though his parents had stayed together while Andrew was growing up, his father had never really been there. Not when it mattered. Pursuing the Noble legacy—making money—had crowded out everything else in Theodore Noble's life.

When Andrew was thirteen, his father had worked his way into a fatal heart attack, leaving behind business associates instead of friends...and a family who grieved his passing, not only because they were going to miss him but because they'd never really known him in the first place.

When Andrew had turned eighteen, the terms of his father's will had opened the valve to his trust fund.

And he'd started a new legacy.

Chapter Three

"Are you sure you're all right? Hallie said you took a pretty good spill." Miranda's fingers ran over her son's bony shoulders, down his arms and then altered their course to tickle his ribs.

"Mom!" Daniel giggled and squirmed away, almost falling from his perch on one of the stools at the counter.

"I'm sure it's nothing a sundae won't cure. Isn't that right, Danny Boy?" With a flourish, Isaac presented an old-fashioned soda glass filled with vanilla ice cream. A cloud of whipped cream and a maraschino cherry topped it off.

"Can I have it, Mom?" Daniel's eyes sparkled and Miranda nodded. She knew better than to protest. Both Isaac and Sandra loved to spoil Daniel and she let them, even if it was close to dinnertime.

"Daniel, you keep Isaac company for a few minutes. I've got one more table to take care of and then we can go to the park."

"Okay." Daniel dug in with his spoon, using it to tunnel toward the rich pocket of hot fudge visible at the bottom of the glass.

Miranda fisted her hands in the pockets of her apron to stop them from shaking and went into the kitchen. Sandra stood at the island, deftly cutting up the colorful assortment of vegetables that went into her famous chicken pot pie. She smiled when she saw Miranda.

"Did Dr. Tubman administer the correct dose of hot fudge?"

Miranda felt tears sting the backs of her eyes and blinked them away before Sandra noticed.

"Isaac knows that ice cream cures just about everything that ails a seven-year-old boy."

Sandra paused to study her. Miranda held her breath and met the older woman's gaze straight on. Not that a show of confidence would fool Sandra. She had inner radar that immediately picked up any signs of distress and right now Miranda could tell it had moved to red alert.

"Are you sure everything's all right?" Sandra asked softly. "You look a little upset."

Miranda hesitated. She never wanted to burden her employer with her problems. Even if a picture of Sandra Lange appeared in the dictionary next to the word *nurturer.*

Over the past four years, Sandra had continually reached out to her in friendship while Miranda did her best to keep their relationship strictly that of employer and employee. It wasn't easy. There'd been times Miranda had wanted to fall into Sandra's plump arms and howl like a baby, knowing the older woman understood what it was like to have to live with the consequences of your mistakes. What it felt like to have God pull the rug out from under you.

As a young woman, Sandra had fallen in love with the wrong man, too. He'd deceived her and taken their infant daughter away. Even though Ross Van Zandt, the private investigator Sandra had hired, had discovered Kelly Young was her child, she'd been cheated out of thirty-four years with her. But somehow Sandra refused to dwell on those lost years—she only counted every minute she had with Kelly now as precious.

During that same time, Miranda had watched Sandra fight breast cancer and come out victorious. The effects of chemo had ravaged Sandra's body but never her faith. In fact, the battle with cancer had somehow seemed to *strengthen* her relationship with God. That was what Miranda couldn't understand. Her own experience with God hadn't been like that at all.

She'd accepted Christ as a teenager at a youth event in her hometown and over the next few years, her faith had slowly taken root. Until Lorraine and Tom had been killed in a car accident. Losing her older sister and brother-in-law one New Year's Eve to a drunk driver had tipped her world upside down. So had becoming a single parent. And she hadn't known what to hold on to.

According to her pastor, she was supposed to cling to God, but He wasn't flesh and blood. God couldn't comfort Daniel when he cried for his parents. Or walk him around the room when he was sick with the flu. God couldn't sit down and have a cup of coffee with her and ask her about her day.

But Hal Stevens could.

She'd turned to Hal for strength. For love. To ease the loneliness that crept into her days. She'd had no idea he would begin to turn the qualities she'd been drawn to into weapons.

Which was why, when it came right down to it, she couldn't confide in Sandra. It was pointless. No one could rescue her. No one could change her past. God wouldn't waste His time on someone who'd messed up the way she had.

"Miranda?" Sandra's voice gently drew her back to reality, nudging her away from the shadowy path her memories always took her down.

"Just a little glitch." Miranda realized she needed to put Sandra's mind at ease so she deliberately kept her voice light. "When Hallie dropped Daniel off, she reminded me that she has gymnastics camp next week. I don't remember her mentioning it before but she insists she did. Either way, I'll have to find someone else to watch him."

Miranda didn't bring up the fact that she had no idea who she could get to take care of Daniel on such short notice. Or that she was a little frustrated with Daniel's babysitter. When she'd interviewed her, the young teen had seemed enthusiastic about earning some spending money. Miranda had assumed Hallie's enthusiasm would extend to what she was doing to *earn* the money, which was take care of a quiet, good-natured little boy for four to five hours during the day. But judging from innocent comments Daniel had made lately, it sounded as if Hallie had a lot of friends. And an unlimited number of cell-phone minutes.

If Miranda couldn't be with Daniel all the time, she needed to have confidence in the person who was. And she wasn't sure, anymore, that it was Hallie.

Sandra wiped her hands on a towel and closed her eyes, humming one of the praise songs she enjoyed listening to while they worked. Miranda knew Sandra wasn't ignoring her—she was praying.

The stab of envy she felt surprised her. She wanted that kind of peace. The kind of peace that made a person smile even if everything around her was falling apart.

Sandra's eyes popped open and the look on her face made Miranda wonder if God really *had* said something to her. "I have an idea."

"What is it?" Miranda asked cautiously, not sure if she should trust the sparkle in Sandra's eyes.

"Sonshine Camp is next week." She said the words confidently, as if Miranda was supposed to know what she was talking about.

She let her confusion show. "I've never heard of that."

"At church. It's from eight to noon. Daniel could come to work with you for an hour and then go over to the church. When it's finished, he can come back and have lunch here at the diner. Your shift ends at one, so it'll work out perfectly."

Miranda should have known Sandra's solution would have something to do with Chestnut Grove Community Church. An active member of the congregation, Sandra counted Reverend Fraser and his wife, Naomi, as close friends. She frequently referred to the people who attended Chestnut Grove Community as "the family God gave her."

"We don't belong to your church." Miranda voiced the first excuse she could come up with.

"It isn't just for our members—it's for the entire community. Haven't you seen the flyers up everywhere? Pastor Caleb's youth group is organizing it this year. Anne has been working on craft projects and some of the men are volunteering to help with games. I think they're even going to play baseball."

Miranda wavered. Daniel loved baseball. He didn't play on a youth league but he collected cards and had memorized a mind-boggling number of batting averages and player statistics.

"How much does it cost?" She hadn't budgeted for camp and an entire week would probably be more than she could afford. Especially when Daniel needed new clothes.

Sandra chuckled. "Not a thing, honey. It's free."

"Free?" Miranda couldn't help the skepticism that leaked into the word.

"The church sponsors this as an outreach to the community. Pastor Caleb and Anne have a heart for this town…and for kids."

Miranda couldn't argue with that. It seemed as if whenever she saw Caleb and Anne Williams, they were surrounded by children, ranging in age from their six-month-old daughter, Christina Rose, to the teenagers who made up the church's youth group. Right after they'd gotten married, they'd adopted Dylan, one of the boys in Caleb's youth group who'd been in foster care. It wouldn't be a stretch to imagine the couple volunteering their time and energy to a weeklong children's camp.

"I don't know." Miranda still wasn't sure she should

let Daniel participate. Over the past few years she'd deliberately kept their lives private. It was easier to keep her distance than to let people get close enough to ask questions she couldn't answer.

"You can't say no. This has God's signature on it," Sandra said, her unshakable faith evident in her cheerful tone.

"I can't leave work to drive him there and it's too far to walk." Her final, feeble excuse.

Sandra winked. "You leave that to me. We'll get Daniel there if I have to drive him myself."

Judging from the number of cars parked in Eli and Rachel's driveway, Andrew figured the word about Rachel's condition had gotten out.

He hauled a large white bag stuffed with gift-wrapped packages out of the passenger side of his Ferrari. It contained the ice cream he'd promised and a few things he hoped would make Rachel smile. A CD player with two sets of headphones—one for her and one for baby—and a collection of instrumental lullabies to go along with it. A pair of knitting needles. Gold, of course. He'd stuck them in a ball of funky blue yarn that had reminded him of a poodle. One that had come unraveled. Then, so she couldn't accuse him of favoring the masculine gender, he'd bought one in raspberry-pink, too.

He knocked at the door and it opened quickly to reveal a pert little face. Ben and Leah Cavanaugh's daughter, Olivia. Ben and Rachel's husband, Eli, were brothers so that made the Cavanaughs *family* as far as Andrew was concerned.

"Is there room for one more?" he whispered.

Olivia recognized him immediately and giggled, opening the door. "We brought lasagna for Aunt Rachel."

"Looks like I'm right on time, then."

"Come on." Without an ounce of shyness, Olivia grabbed his hand and towed him into the foyer. "They're in the living room."

The conversation stalled when Andrew appeared in the doorway. Rachel was stretched out on the leather sofa and Eli sat at her feet. Or more likely, Andrew thought, he was sitting *on* them so she couldn't get up. Ben stood in front of the fireplace, his infant son, Joseph, cradled in his arms. He must have come over straight from work because he still wore the denim shirt with the logo for Cavanaugh Carpentry embroidered on the pocket. Judging from the sounds coming from the kitchen, Andrew guessed Ben's wife, Leah, was the one putting dinner together.

Rachel spied the bag. "Is there ice cream in there?"

"Enough to last a day or two. How are you doing?" He wandered close enough to see the fine lines etched at the corners of her eyes.

Rachel pursed her lips. "I've been lying on this sofa for six hours, twelve minutes and..." She glanced at her diamond wristwatch. "Fourteen seconds. What does that tell you?"

"Mmm. That you're going crazy?"

"And bringing Eli along for the ride." Rachel cast an apologetic glance at her husband.

"I told you I'd follow you anywhere." He grinned.

The look that passed between them momentarily

blocked out everyone else in the room. Andrew felt a jab of envy. He could pick up the phone and have a dinner date within the hour. He could spend an evening laughing with a woman and making casual conversation, but it never progressed beyond that. He was thirty-four years old and he'd never dated a woman he wanted to share his heart—and his life—with. He was beginning to think she didn't exist.

"Dinner is served." Leah Cavanaugh swept into the room like a tawny-haired sunbeam, holding a beautifully carved tray crowded with delicate china and garnished with a single red rose.

Andrew watched her set it down on the coffee table next to Rachel and his thoughts drifted back to Miranda. For the second or third…or hundredth…time that day.

He had enough secrets of his own to be able to recognize them in someone else's eyes. It made him curious. What was her story? Why was she cautious around men?

Maybe she isn't cautious around men. Maybe she's just cautious around you….

He didn't have time to dwell on that thought because Leah took command of the room. Rachel had insisted everyone eat with her instead of in the formal dining room so, in no time, Leah had everyone sitting down, enjoying the meal she'd prepared.

The doorbell rang and Olivia, the unofficial greeter, danced away to answer it. She returned, arm-in-arm, with Jonah Fraser, one of Ben's employees. The little girl carefully matched her steps to Jonah's, who still walked with a slight limp due to an injury during a tour of duty in Iraq.

"Jonah?" Ben strode forward and met him halfway. "What's up?"

"I'm sorry to bother you here, Ben, but—" Jonah looked uncomfortable with the attention his unexpected visit was receiving. "Is there somewhere we can talk?"

"Did you run into problems at the Harcourt mansion today?" Ben asked, a frown of concern creasing in forehead.

"You could say that." Jonah exhaled slowly. It was the only sound in the room because everyone had stopped eating.

"You two can use the library," Rachel offered, her worried gaze moving between the two men.

Leah took Ben's hand, giving him a reassuring smile. He took a step toward Jonah and then paused.

"Jonah, if this has something to do with you, we'll go into the library. If it has something to do with me, you might as well just spill it or I'll get stuck repeating it again. And again. And again."

His attempt at humor fell flat. Everyone could see the tension in Jonah's broad shoulders. He gave Ben a curt nod. "All right. I ripped out a wall at the mansion while I was working in Samantha Harcourt's suite of rooms this afternoon and I found a folder filled with…documents."

Ben's jaw tightened. "What kind of documents?"

"From Tiny Blessings. There's a stack of them at least an inch thick. And…I saw your name."

Ben flinched as if the words had physically struck him. "Documents? From Tiny Blessings? Are you telling me you may have found copies of my adoption records?"

"I'm not sure." Jonah's fists clenched at his sides, the

only visible sign of his frustration. "I think they might be your *original* adoption records, Ben."

Leah sucked in a breath and Ben looked dazed.

"I wanted to tell you first because I know what this could mean. There are a lot of records there. Who knows which ones are legit and which ones are fakes? Either way, they're going to blow another hole in Ross and Kelly's life—and the Harcourts'. Not to mention other families who adopted through the agency and assumed everything was on the up and up. Or—" Jonah hesitated "—people who paid Harcourt to cover their tracks."

Andrew saw the truth of his words begin to sink in on everyone's faces. He'd been living in Rhode Island when the first batch of falsified adoption records had been discovered a few years back. Rachel had confided in him at the time, not only because the Noble Foundation supported Tiny Blessings but because Kelly Young Van Zandt, the director, was one of Rachel's friends.

"Do you… Did you…notice anything else on the papers? The ones that had my name on them?" Ben asked.

Jonah understood the significance of the question and he nodded. "Your mother… Her name was there."

Leah closed her eyes and Ben instinctively drew her and Olivia into the shelter of his arms.

"It's Millicent. Millicent Cunningham."

"Cunningham." Ben repeated the name, trying to keep his emotions under control.

"What do you want me to do?" Jonah asked simply.

Ben was silent. It was Leah who stepped into the gap.

"First we're going to pray," she said. "And then we're going to call Ross."

Chapter Four

"*Pleeease,* Miranda. You're the only person I know who doesn't have plans on a Friday night." Darcy clasped her hands together and probably would have dropped to her knees if she hadn't been wearing her favorite pair of white jeans.

She'd trapped Miranda in the small break room off the kitchen when she'd stopped at the diner to pick up her paycheck.

Miranda wasn't sure what amused her more—the truth in the desperate plea or that Darcy could draw out a simple, one-syllable word like *please* for ten excruciating seconds.

"Just for the record, I do have a date. With a very handsome young man. We're going to play Chutes and Ladders, drink root beer and eat popcorn."

"Sounds boring… Oh, you're talking about *Daniel.*" Darcy looked relieved. "I only need you to cover the last hour of my shift so Greg and I can catch the nine o'clock movie. One hour. That's it. I promise. This could be the night when he falls madly in love with me. My entire future rests in your hands." She nibbled on the tips of her artificial nails and waited while Miranda decided her fate.

"I thought you were waiting for Andrew Noble to fall madly in love with you." Miranda couldn't resist teasing her a little.

"You were right. Andrew might be Mr. Gorgeous and Available to three or four women on this planet, but he's Mr. Gorgeous and Out of My League to Darcy Gibson. Greg drives a brand new Saturn and doesn't live with his mother. I'd say that makes him a pretty good catch, wouldn't you?" She snapped her gum to underscore the point.

"I'll work for you." It was the safest thing Miranda could say at the moment.

Darcy squealed and hugged her. "Thanks, Miranda. I owe you. If you ever have a real date and need someone to keep an eye on Dan the Little Man, let me know. He's into science, right? I remember some cool experiments from chem class."

Miranda made a mental note never to ask Darcy to babysit. Ever. Not that she'd be going out on a date anytime soon. The one serious relationship she'd had in her life, with Hal Stevens, had shaken her to the core. She no longer trusted her own judgment when it came to men.

She had met Hal at the bank where she'd worked as a loans officer and immediately she'd been drawn to him. Good-looking and successful, Hal was a junior partner in a local law firm. His confident, take-charge personality seemed to be just what she'd needed at that time in her life. Reeling from the loss of her beloved older sister and trying to figure out how to parent an active toddler, Miranda had been overwhelmed. Hal'd swept into her life like the proverbial knight on a white horse.

Within months, however, the "take-charge" man who'd lovingly encouraged her to lean on him slowly took over her life. He'd openly criticized her friends until they eventually stopped calling. He'd accused her of flirting with the male customers who came into the bank. He'd dropped in during business hours to check up on her. Somewhere along the way, his attentive courtship had morphed into a jealous obsession. Gradually his tirades weren't only limited to the men Miranda had come into contact with at the bank—they'd started to cast a dark shadow on her relationship with Daniel. Hal had begun to complain about the amount of attention she gave to her son.

Miranda had found herself living in a nightmare. And it got worse. One evening, she'd told Hal she couldn't go to a concert with him because Daniel had a fever. Hal had screamed that Daniel wasn't even her biological son so it wasn't fair he had to compete with the boy. And then he'd pushed her against the wall. It was the first time his attacks had crossed the line from verbal to physical. Daniel had witnessed the scuffle and had burst into tears. It had given Miranda the courage to do what she had to do. She'd broken up with him.

But Hal hadn't been willing to let her go. He wouldn't stop calling her. He'd shown up at the bank where she'd worked. But one evening, when he'd let himself into her apartment with a key she didn't know he'd had, and Miranda knew she had to make a decision.

Less than a week later, she'd taken Daniel and fled from her home in Georgia in the middle of the night. She'd had one suitcase and a vague destination in mind—Chestnut Grove, just outside of Richmond, Virginia. It was as good a place as any for a fresh start and it would take them far away from Hal. Miranda didn't have any roots there but Daniel did. He'd been a newborn when Lorraine and Tom had adopted him from Tiny Blessings Adoption Agency.

Her relationship with Hal had cost her more than her job and her security. It had devastated her ability to trust. And knowing that Hal might still be looking for her—even after four years—kept her constantly on edge.

Not exactly the kind of baggage a woman could carry into a new relationship.

"I know that look." Darcy put her hands on Miranda's shoulders and shook her lightly. "Daniel's dad messed with your head and now you think all men are scum. And they are. The trick is to figure out which ones are *always* going to be scum and which ones have the potential to be descummed."

"I'll remember that." Miranda's reluctant laughter over this latest Darcy-ism chased away the specter of the past.

Encouraged, Darcy warmed to the subject. "You could put a little more effort into your appearance. No offense, but even older women should make the most of what they have. You could put some highlights in your hair and use a little eyeshadow. I found this great color called Astro blue—"

Which, if Miranda remembered correctly, had enough metallic sparkle in it to get her a part as an extra in a sci-fi movie.

"I'll see you tonight at eight, Darcy..." Miranda suddenly noticed one of the buttons on her summer-weight sweater had come loose and was hanging from the placket like a broken spring.

Darcy zeroed in on it. She blew a bubble and let it pop. Just for effect. "My opinion? Don't replace the button, replace the cardigan."

Or I could use it as a muzzle.

"I'll think about it." Miranda escaped to the kitchen before Darcy offered to lend her one of *her* sweaters.

She found Daniel standing next to Isaac, carefully refilling the salt shakers. A swatch of silky brown hair, which needed a trim, flopped over one eye.

"Ready to go, Daniel?"

"You two off to the park today?" Isaac boomed above the hiss of the grill.

"Yup." Daniel nodded vigorously and his glasses slipped down to the end of his nose.

"Hit a couple home runs for me, Danny Boy."

"Daniel doesn't play baseball," Miranda reminded him. "We're going to look for bugs to add to his collection."

"Well, you can keep those things out of my kitchen," Isaac muttered. "Imagine *looking* for bugs. On purpose."

"Will you tell Sandra I'll be back in tonight to close up?" Miranda called over her shoulder. "I'm covering for Darcy."

"Sure thing." Isaac used one hand to flip a pancake and the other to ladle gravy over a plate of biscuits. "Order up!"

"We could play baseball. If you want to," Daniel said as Miranda ushered him out the back door into the alley where he'd parked his bicycle.

"Bug collecting is fine with me." Miranda ruffled his hair. "I know you don't like to play."

"Okay." The toe of Daniel's shoe scuffed at the dirt.

Miranda slanted a look at him. "Everything all right?"

"Yeah." He hopped on his bicycle and Miranda stared at it in disbelief. She'd bought it on clearance two summers ago and it suddenly looked way too small for him.

Daniel was growing up too fast.

He needs a dad.

The thought came out of nowhere and blindsided her. She sucked in a ragged breath. Hadn't she just been reliving how horrible their lives had been when she'd let Hal in? Her loneliness and vulnerability had made her a target for his manipulative personality. By trying to fill a void, she'd only ended up creating a larger one.

If she could be tricked so easily by one man, what would stop her from being tricked again?

It wasn't worth the risk.

Andrew had a nine o'clock dinner reservation. And a sudden craving for apple pie. This would send François, the head chef at his favorite restaurant, into a culinary tantrum if he even said the words out loud. He'd end up with some puff-pastry thing the size of quarter with a slice of apple inside it that didn't even look like an apple. Because it *wouldn't be* an apple. It would be something more acceptable—like a pomegranate.

Only one place served honest-to-goodness-homemade-with-a-flaky-crust-and-oozing-with-real-apples apple pie. And it happened to be less than ten minutes away from the apartment. He'd still be on time for his dinner reservation—he just wouldn't have to order dessert.

"Andrew!" Sandra greeted him warmly when he walked into the diner. She sat at the counter next to Isaac, a cup of coffee cradled in her hands. "Are you here for a late supper or something sweet?"

He resisted the urge to scan the dining room to see if Miranda was there. Not that he *expected* to see her. She'd worked the breakfast and lunch shift both times he'd eaten at the diner.

But a guy can hope....

It was worse than he'd thought. When had he become such a glutton for punishment? He had a knack for reading people and Miranda's cool reserve stated loud and clear that she wanted to be left alone.

He glanced at the empty stools lining the counter. Tonight, he didn't want to be the high-maintenance playboy. Not with Sandra and Isaac. "It looks like you're closing soon."

"Not for an hour. The grill's still hot," Isaac rumbled.

Andrew wondered what Chef François would say about the Starlight Diner's gruff old cook. Tufts of white hair formed an uneven strip around the circumference of Isaac's head and matched the eyebrows sprouting on both sides of a caricature of a nose. The stained, tarplike apron he wore didn't quite cover the belly spilling over the top of his baggy pants. Pants held up by bright red suspenders.

He decided the two men would be trading recipes and good-natured insults within five minutes.

"Don't mind us, we're not usually this lazy," Sandra said, patting the stool next to her as an invitation for Andrew to sit down. "The local news just ran a segment on our favorite hometown celebrity, Douglas Matthews. They're saying his talk show has a shot at going national. That would certainly put Chestnut Grove on the map."

"It's already on the map," Isaac muttered, but Andrew noticed his eyes were glued to the television and there was a hint of pride in his voice.

"Douglas is homegrown. I'm sure if his show is picked up by one of the big networks, we'll be the first ones to know," Sandra said. "Now, don't be shy, Andrew. What can I get you?"

He decided honesty was the best policy. "Actually, I was hoping for a piece of your apple pie."

"I think we have some in the kitchen—"

"I'll get it."

Andrew heard Miranda's voice behind him and realized she must have been there all along. She wore her pink waitress uniform with her hair still scraped away from her face in a sedate twist, but now a pair of tortoiseshell glasses perched on her nose. On anyone else they might have looked severe, but on Miranda, they created a worthy frame for the velvet brown eyes. She looked beautiful. And fascinating.

"Thank you—"

Before he could finish the sentence, the doors between the kitchen and the dining room swished shut.

All right, then.

Even Isaac looked a little confused by her abrupt departure. With an apologetic glance at Andrew, he lumbered to his feet and followed her into the kitchen.

"Miranda was a finance major so she handles the books for the diner," Sandra told him. "She's covering for Darcy tonight but it's been slow the last half hour so she's juggling numbers instead."

A finance major? Interesting.

"So the diner is part-time?" He deliberately kept his voice casual, not wanting to admit, even to himself, how curious he was about Miranda Jones's personal life.

"No." Sandra shook her head. "She used to work at a bank but she told me she prefers to waitress. That's a blessing for me—she's one of my best employees."

Something about that bit of information struck Andrew as odd. Not the part about Miranda being a good employee but that she preferred to be a waitress. A bank definitely offered more in the way of advancement. Not to mention a higher wage. Before he could question Sandra further, Miranda returned with a slab of apple pie that sentenced him to an extra set of stomach crunches in the gym tomorrow.

Instead of looking directly at him, her gaze found a focal point over his shoulder.

"Would you like ice cream?"

"Sure." Make it two sets.

She stood close enough for him to smell her perfume. It was a light floral fragrance, delicate and tantalizing. A totally unexpected bolt of attraction skidded through him.

Whoa.

He did what came naturally when confronted by a

problem. He immediately turned to God to help him sort through it.

What is this, Lord? I don't know anything about Miranda Jones. And she sure doesn't act like she wants to get to know me....

"I'll be right back." She managed a polite smile and slipped behind the counter where a small freezer was located.

See what I mean?

Sandra leaned closer and lowered her voice. "Kelly told me about the documents Jonah found at the mansion yesterday. Ross started to sort through them today but it's going to be a huge undertaking. He said the dates on some of them go back ten years."

The ice-cream scoop in Miranda's hand suddenly clattered to the floor.

"I'm sorry," she murmured, kneeling down to retrieve it.

Andrew frowned as he watched her. The color had drained from her cheeks, leaving her eyes huge in her heart-shaped face and dark with an emotion he couldn't decipher. Embarrassment? That wouldn't make sense. No. It had almost looked like *fear.*

Sandra's hand covered his, pulling his attention back to their conversation. Tears gathered in her eyes before she could blink them away.

"Kelly has worked so hard to restore Tiny Blessings' reputation after the damage Barnaby Harcourt caused," she said softly. "I can't believe she has to go through this again. Not to mention all the families who could be affected by these new documents Jonah found. I trust that

God knows what He's doing, but I can't help but wonder why so many people have to suffer the consequences of one man's greed."

It didn't surprise Andrew that Kelly Young Van Zandt had confided in Sandra. Kelly's husband, Ross, was the private investigator Sandra had hired to find the child she'd given up years ago, so he was also the one who'd discovered that Kelly Young was Sandra's biological daughter. The relationship between the two women had had a rocky start but now they were extremely close. Another testimony to God's goodness.

"According to Eli and Rachel, Ben tried to find his birth mother but eventually he'd hit a dead end," Andrew said. "If Ross has enough information to find her now, maybe Ben's questions will be answered and something good will come out of this mess."

"What man meant for evil, God meant for good," Sandra quoted. Her eyes sparkled, but not from tears this time. "You're right. Come to think of it, I'm living, breathing proof of that promise."

So am I.

Andrew didn't say the words out loud but the truth in them flooded him with a familiar sense of peace. The peace that had carried him through the most traumatic experience of his life.

"That's what I'm going to pray for," Sandra declared, striking her hand on the counter for emphasis. "That God is going to somehow shine His light into the darkness Barnaby Harcourt created."

Andrew silently added some new names to his prayer list. Ross and Kelly. Ben. Especially Ben. Everyone had witnessed how shaken up he'd been by Jonah's discovery. He was closer than ever to unraveling the mystery surrounding his birth and it would take a lot of strength to follow a path with no guarantee where it would end.

Miranda had unobtrusively deposited the pie and ice cream in front of him while he and Sandra had talked, but instead of going back to the booth in the corner to work on the books, she lingered behind the counter, straightening items on the shelves.

Even focused on Sandra, Andrew was acutely aware of her presence. Some of her color had returned but she still seemed fragile. What had upset her? The surge of protectiveness he felt startled him as much as that first jolt of mind-numbing attraction had.

Sandra must have caught something in his expression because she glanced over her shoulder and saw Miranda. A faint smile scooped out the dimple in her cheek.

"Oh, sugar, I should have been paying attention. It's after nine. Let me and Isaac clean up. You have to get home."

Andrew winced. Nine o'clock. He'd totally forgotten his dinner reservation. Forgiveness wasn't exactly high on the temperamental chef's list of qualities, either. Oh, well. Five minutes of drama spewed out in French was worth the unexpected bonus of seeing Miranda again.

Miranda looked torn. "I can stay a few more minutes. I'm sure Daniel won't mind."

Daniel?

His gaze automatically slid to Miranda's left hand.

No ring circled her finger. Not that that meant anything these days.

Disappointment crashed over him. Maybe this was the answer to his prayer. God was telling him that Miranda Jones wasn't available. Because whomever Daniel was, he was obviously significant. There was love in her eyes when she said the name.

Chapter Five

The man had come back.

Somewhere above his head, the tread of heavy footsteps paced the floor, muffling the drone of a television. Darkness crowded him. The kind of darkness that closed in like a thick fog, swallowing every bit of light. Trying to swallow *him.* He could feel the man's rage pulse through the house, seeping into the damp cracks in the walls that surrounded him.

Nowhere to hide. Any moment, the door would be flung open, allowing a rush of light in. Allowing the man to see him huddled in the corner.

No escape. No escape…

Andrew jackknifed in bed, sweat beading out of every pore. As his gaze bounced around the room, the stifling darkness gradually gave way to familiar shapes. The chair in the corner. The outline of the wardrobe where he'd hung up his suit the day before.

He sank back against the pillows, weary and wrung

out. As if he'd fought a battle instead of simply falling asleep. He closed his eyes and took deep, even breaths until his heart stopped slamming against his chest and settled into a normal pattern. The nightmare hadn't plagued him for more than three months. Why now?

Finish the story, Andrew. That wasn't the end of it.

Andrew managed a smile as the words swept through him, removing the last traces of the nightmare.

You know what happened, Lord.

Silence. He chuckled. It was just like God to nudge him back into the memory so he wouldn't be trapped in the black hole of his past. So he would remember he'd come out on the other side of that traumatic experience, his faith forged by the reality that God *was*. That He loved him.

Obediently, Andrew played through the rest of the silent tape. When fear had become as real as the darkness and had tried to suck the breath from his lungs, he'd put his hands together and had opened them like a book. He'd imagined turning the pages, telling himself the stories from the children's Bible his grandmother had given him the week before. On his fifth birthday.

Has your God been able to rescue you?

Just like Daniel in the lion's den, he'd been able to say yes.

There you go, Lord. The end of the story.

But in many ways, the beginning.

His eyes snapped open when his cell phone rang. A special ring tone that immediately caught his attention. The haze of sleep evaporated as he flipped it open.

"Hello?" His voice broke the silence, as clear and sharp as if it were the middle of the day.

"Terrance McCauslin. Miami," a voice rasped the cryptic words in his ear.

"I'm listening." Andrew sprang out of bed and padded to his laptop. He typed in his password.

GUARDIAN.

"Miranda, honey, thank goodness you're back. You'd think the entire town smelled Isaac's homemade sausage and decided to come out for breakfast this morning. Table six needs menus and table five needs a warm-up on his coffee." Sandra fanned herself with an oven mitt and chuckled. "It's Monday. Definitely."

Sandra was the only person Miranda knew who could have half a dozen things go wrong the minute the diner opened and still be able to waltz serenely around the kitchen.

The deliveryman who dropped off the dairy order every morning hadn't shown up, so Sandra had sent Miranda to the grocery store to purchase enough whipping cream to hold them over until he arrived.

She set the package down and slipped off her sweater. The one Darcy had suggested she retire. Instead, she'd fixed the button.

"Look, Mom! Isaac is letting me flip the pancakes all by myself!" Daniel called to her from his station by the grill, wrapped up like a mummy in an apron three sizes too big for him.

Miranda forced a smile. Too bad Sandra's serenity couldn't be bottled and sold like the whipping cream she'd bought. The conversation she'd overheard between Sandra and Andrew had kept her awake the past two nights.

Two years ago, she'd almost taken Daniel and left Chestnut Grove in the wake of the scandal at Tiny Blessings. Even though she trusted Daniel's adoption had been perfectly legal, so had many other people who'd found out just the opposite. Barnaby Harcourt's blackmail schemes were all the customers had talked about for months. Fortunately, when Sandra had hired her, Sandra, like everyone else, had assumed Daniel was Miranda's son. With their brown hair and eyes, they even looked alike.

She took comfort in the fact no one knew Daniel had originally been adopted through Tiny Blessings. And even though Kelly's husband, Ross, had begun the painstaking process of sorting through falsified birth certificates and adoption records, Miranda had decided the best thing was to stay in Chestnut Grove to keep an eye on his findings.

She'd finally started to let her guard down and now this. She couldn't—*wouldn't*—lose Daniel.

"I know someone who's going to have a job here in a few years," Sandra said, pausing to drop a kiss on the top of Daniel's head.

If we're still here.

Some people, Miranda knew—like Darcy—had their lives planned out for the next fifty years. Miranda had learned to accept she couldn't be that kind of person. Experience had taught her that she couldn't trust tomorrow. It shifted like a sandbar, leaving her scrambling for something solid.

"Look at this one," Daniel said. "It's not very round but Isaac says that's okay."

"You're doing great, Daniel." Miranda couldn't help responding to the excitement in her son's voice. She knew that flipping pancakes wasn't the only reason Daniel had popped out of bed with a smile on his face that morning.

It was the first day of Sonshine Camp and Daniel had been thrilled when she'd told him he could spend an hour with her at the diner before leaving for the church.

True to her word, Sandra had found a ride for Daniel. Leah Cavanaugh's daughter, Olivia, planned to attend the day camp, too. Leah had assured Miranda when she'd called the night before that it was no trouble to pick up Daniel on her way.

"It's almost time for you to go, Daniel," she reminded him. "You should watch out the window for Mrs. Cavanaugh."

"I think he should stay here and help me this morning," Isaac said. "He'll be a short-order cook in no time."

"Can I take it out?" Daniel asked eagerly.

"Sure can. You made them," Isaac said before Miranda could protest. "Let me slide these eggs on the plate—gotta be careful so the yolks don't break. Now grab the tray with both hands. Steady. There you go."

Miranda followed Daniel through the doors, catching them before they swung back and knocked him over.

In the twenty minutes she'd been gone, the diner had filled to capacity.

Oh, no. Miranda's heart smacked against her rib cage. Andrew Noble sat in the booth by the window. In her section. Again. He was on his way to becoming a permanent fixture at the diner. Or, at least, one of their "regulars."

She stifled a groan, still uncertain about the strange mixture of feelings the sight of him stirred in her.

He was scanning the morning edition of the *Gazette*, oblivious to covert glances from female customers.

"Hey, Miranda! Can I get a couple of those blueberry muffins to go?" A woman in running clothes waved her napkin to get Miranda's attention. Unfortunately, she got Daniel's attention, too. He turned slightly and the tray wobbled. Instead of pausing to adjust to the shift in weight, he kept moving forward, which sent the heavy stoneware plate on a downward course toward the end of the tray.

Miranda, only a few steps behind him, saw exactly what was about to happen but was powerless to stop it. The plate bumped against the edge of the tray and the food kept going. Three buttermilk pancakes and two eggs over easy went airborne. And landed on Andrew Noble's shoes.

"Mom!" Daniel whispered the word and the terrified look on his face brought her quickly to his side. She wrapped her arm around his trembling shoulders and gave him a comforting squeeze.

"It's okay, Daniel," she murmured. "It was an accident."

Which was the truth, although she wasn't sure if a man like Andrew Noble would see it from that perspective. Especially when the accident involved egg yolks and Italian leather.

When she gathered her courage to look at Andrew, he was staring at them with an inscrutable look on his face. Then, he grinned.

"Ah...*Daniel?* I've decided to change my order. I'd like my eggs scrambled, please."

Then he gave Daniel a cheerful wink.

Pure, unadulterated relief coursed through Andrew. He'd just flown in from Florida an hour ago, where he'd spent a grueling twenty-four hours stuffed in the back of an unair-conditioned van while he'd tried to pinpoint the destination of an unpredictable ex-con and a frightened six-year-old.

That particular story had had a happy ending but he hadn't stayed to witness it. He never did. There were people who tied up the loose ends for him and smiled for the six o'clock news team. It was enough for him just to *know.*

At the moment, adrenaline and a Thermos of the pilot's coffee he'd had earlier—so thick with coffee grounds he'd been tempted to ask for a fork—were the only things keeping him awake.

His plan had been to shower, change his clothes and report for duty at the Foundation. Instead, he'd sat in his car outside the Starlight Diner for fifteen minutes, debating whether or not he should go inside. He was pathetic. Torn between wanting to see Miranda and having to face the fact she might be in a committed relationship with a guy named Daniel.

And she was.

Except the Daniel waiting for Miranda to come home on Friday night was her *son.*

Even without swim goggles covering most of the serious little face, Andrew immediately recognized the boy whose towel he'd pulled out of the bicycle chain a few days ago. And now that the two were side by side, he could see the faint resemblance.

Both had glossy brown hair and delicate features almost eclipsed by enormous brown eyes, but while Miranda's held fascinating glints of gold, Daniel's were as dark as espresso.

Even though he'd tried to defuse the tension with humor, both pairs of eyes were still fixed on him. And filled with apprehension.

"Daniel…run and get a bucket and a rag from Isaac," Miranda murmured.

She pulled a cache of napkins out of her apron pocket and looked down at his shoes, her intention clear.

Not in this lifetime.

"I'll take care of it, Miranda." Andrew reached out and caught her hand. He hadn't meant to sound so abrupt but he couldn't understand the fear radiating from her. What did she expect him to do? Shout "Off with their heads"?

Miranda yanked her hand away.

"I'm sorry, Mr. Noble. Daniel loves to help in the kitchen and…well, I'll pay to have your shoes cleaned or replaced."

She'd just insulted him and didn't even know it. Andrew drew in a breath and released it. Slowly. "That's not necessary. It was an accident."

Daniel returned with the bucket and Andrew gave him another smile as he gently removed it from the boy's hands. Miranda made a sound of protest. He ignored her.

"I didn't know you worked here, Daniel." He unbuttoned his cuffs and pushed his sleeves back. It only took three efficient swipes to remove the goo from his shoes. He lowered his voice to a whisper. "Or is this a cover?"

"My *mom* works here." Daniel giggled.

He'd obviously remembered Andrew, too, and he didn't look as scared as he had a few minutes ago.

"How are the knees? All healed up?"

"Better." Daniel hiked up the hems of his cargo shorts a few inches to let Andrew inspect them.

"They look pretty good."

Miranda frowned at him, her expression wary. "How did you—"

"I happened to be there when his beach towel and his bicycle chain decided to get acquainted," Andrew explained.

Daniel nodded vigorously. "He got it unstuck."

"Oh." Miranda caught her full lower lip between her teeth while she processed that unexpected news.

"Miranda?" Sandra hurried over to them, her round cheeks flushed with color from all the activity in the diner. "Leah's waiting outside."

Andrew watched Miranda scrub an invisible speck of dirt off Daniel's chin while he stood as still as a statue and took it like a man. Andrew remembered his mom doing the same thing. "Be good today," she said. "And have fun. Mrs. Cavanaugh is bringing you back here when camp is over, so be sure to watch for her."

Andrew gave Daniel a thumbs-up sign behind Miranda's back, as he took off his apron and grabbed his backpack.

"Okay, Mom." Daniel gave Andrew another shy

smile before darting away, his backpack bouncing with every step.

"He'll have a great time," Sandra reassured Miranda as Leah waved to them from the other side of the window.

"I know. It's all he could talk about over the weekend."

"Sonshine Camp," Andrew guessed.

Her eyes widened in surprise and he shrugged. "I got an e-mail from Caleb Williams. He needed a few more volunteers this week."

"I'll have to call Anne and ask her if there's anything I can do." Sandra jotted a note to herself on the back of her order pad. "And Andrew, I'll bring you another pancake special. On the house."

She bustled away but Miranda lingered. At least she wasn't running in the opposite direction. If sacrificing a pair of shoes got her to talk to him, he wasn't about to complain.

"Thank you for not yelling at Daniel," she finally said.

He frowned. What kind of jerk did she think he was?

"They're just shoes, Miranda."

He saw it then. The shadow that darkened her eyes told him there'd been someone in Daniel's life who wouldn't have seen it that way.

His stomach tightened.

Daniel's father?

The thought of anyone mistreating Miranda and her son sent a surge of anger coursing through him. He quickly conquered it. If he wanted to convince Miranda Jones that she shouldn't lump all men into the same category with the man who'd hurt her, he had to win her over with something she wasn't used to receiving.

Understanding.

Miranda froze, struck by the compassion she saw in Andrew's eyes. As if her words had somehow given him access to her heart and he could see the damage there.

Damage caused by trusting the wrong man.

Look at him, Miranda. His eyes are bloodshot and he didn't even take time to shave this morning. It's obvious he's been up all night. And he probably wasn't alone….

"I have to get back to work." Miranda grabbed the bucket and escaped to the kitchen.

She wasn't going to think about Andrew Noble. Or talk about Andrew Noble….

"Andrew is a sweetheart, isn't he?"

Miranda's mouth fell open as Sandra coasted past her, a knowing smile on her face.

"A *sweetheart?*" She almost choked on the word.

"I could see he's got a soft spot for children, couldn't you?"

No, Miranda wanted to shout. But then she remembered the friendly wink he'd given Daniel. And the serious appraisal of his skinned knees.

"Maybe." Reluctant, but the best she could do.

"And Kelly mentioned how much Rachel appreciates him taking over the Foundation while she's on bed rest," Sandra continued, an innocent twinkle in her eyes.

In between jaunts to Monaco and St. Bart's.

"I suppose." He had come to help. She couldn't deny it.

"Loyalty." Sandra gave a brisk nod. "It's a good quality and one you don't see often enough these days."

Sure it was. In a golden retriever. With his ink-black hair and lethal smile, Andrew reminded her more of a predator than a docile house pet.

"I've got to take this out." Miranda reached for the plate of pancakes on the pass-through, stifling a groan when she realized she'd picked up the replica of Andrew's first breakfast.

Isaac lifted a brow at Sandra when the doors closed behind Miranda.

"You aren't matchmaking, are you?" he asked suspiciously. "'Cause you and I both know that young lady's hiding some awful hurts."

Sandra pretended to be shocked. "I'd never do that."

Isaac didn't look convinced. "Why not?"

"Because I never try to get in the Lord's way, that's why not. And I have a hunch He's got something of His own in the works."

Chapter Six

You reap what you sow.

The words came back to Ross as he surveyed the papers fanned out on his desk in a spare office at Tiny Blessings.

They were true enough for Barnaby Harcourt. The man had been without a conscience and in the end he'd paid for the web of deceit he'd created. With his life.

Ross knew it wasn't his place to judge, but faced with another batch of evidence of the man's greed, anger coiled in his chest. Because of Harcourt, a lot of innocent people were going to have their lives changed. Some for the better and some for the worse.

There was a light rap on the door and Eric Pellegrino, Tiny Blessings' assistant director, poked his head in. "Ben Cavanaugh is here. He said you wanted to talk to him."

Ross rose to his feet. At least, in Ben's case, it might be for the better. But even that depended on the woman who was going about her life, not knowing she was a phone call away from coming face-to-face with her past.

"Ross." Ben stretched out his calloused hand and shook Ross's over the desk. "I got your message."

"Did Leah come with you?" Ross had been hoping Ben's wife had come along. Ben's faith, like his own, had grown over the past few years but Ross still didn't know what he'd do without Kelly's loving wisdom in his life. He figured it was the same way for Ben and Leah.

Ben shook his head. "She's volunteering at Sonshine Camp this week. I left a voice mail on her phone, but I decided to swing by as soon as I could."

Ross understood. He'd tried unsuccessfully to track down Ben's biological mother until two years ago, when Ben had finally told him he should concentrate on some of the other families whose records Barnaby had changed. Ross knew it had cost Ben a lot to give up the search and hoped what he had to tell him now would make up for it.

So far, word hadn't leaked to the press about the documents Jonah had discovered but Ross knew it was only a matter of time. Jared Kierney, a reporter for the *Gazette*, had found out and was champing at the bit to get the story out. Meg, Jared's wife, was the only reason he'd agreed to sit on it for a while. Over the past few years, Kelly had been absorbed into Meg's group of friends, who met at the Starlight for brunch every Sunday.

"I take it you found something."

Ben's not-so-subtle prompt pushed him back on track.

"What Jonah found was a copy of your original birth certificate. According to the records, your mother's maiden name is Cunningham. I did a little digging over the weekend and from what I've been able to find out, she was a college student when you were born." Ross sighed. This was where things got sticky. "Have you heard of Cunningham Publishing?"

Ben was silent for a few seconds and then shook his head. "No."

"It's a Christian publishing house in Maryland. The Cunningham family is very conservative—and very well known. Your mother was an English major when you were born."

Ben connected the dots quickly. "She was supposed to get involved in the family business. And I got in the way."

"Don't jump to conclusions," Ross cautioned. "Let's just say, for now, that Millicent somehow heard of Barnaby Harcourt, who placed you with your parents. It could be, Harcourt changed your records—for his usual price—and then started to blackmail her. Millicent eventually married a man named Ralph Watson. They have four children together."

Ben sucked in a breath. Strange. In the search for his birth mother, he'd never considered he might have siblings.

"Ralph Watson." Ben repeated the name. "I wonder if he knows about…me."

Ross moved some papers on his desk and handed one to Ben. "Here's your chance to find out. This is the phone number. The Watsons still live in Maryland."

She didn't miss him.

It was impossible to miss someone you didn't know.

"I wonder where Andrew's been the past few days," Sandra said.

Miranda tore her gaze away from the empty booth by the window and felt her cheeks get warm, wondering if Sandra could read her thoughts. "I have no idea. I guess I hadn't thought about it."

Sandra hid a smile. "Is Daniel enjoying camp?"

"He can't stop talking about it. Yesterday, he brought home a plaster cast of his handprint. If he memorizes the verses that go along with the crafts, he gets a special prize at the end of the week."

"So which verse did he memorize yesterday?"

It may have been Daniel's verse but the words had lodged in Miranda's memory, too, lingering at the edges of her thoughts all morning. Knowing Sandra wouldn't let her off the hook, she gave in.

"See, I have engraved you on the palms of my hands."

"Isaiah 49:16." Sandra nodded and closed her eyes, as if savoring the words. "I love that verse. It was one of my promise verses—the verses that comforted me—when I went through chemotherapy."

"But didn't you feel like God had forgotten you?" Miranda asked before she could stop herself.

"Of course there were times I felt that way," Sandra said. "But that's the beauty of a promise, sweetie. No matter how I felt, I leaned on the truth of His word. He wouldn't forget me. He *can't* forget me." She held her palms out. "I'm right *here*."

Miranda felt a stir of longing at the absolute certainty in Sandra's eyes. Daniel was a sensitive boy and it hadn't been enough to simply memorize the verse he'd been given. He'd wanted to know more about the

Bible. Who wrote it? Were the stories true? She'd run out of answers way before he'd stopped asking questions. Finally, caught somewhere between guilt and exasperation, she'd managed to distract him by telling him they could go for a bike ride and feed the ducks at Winchester Park.

"So what do you have planned for your afternoon off?" Sandra asked.

Miranda was grateful for the change in topic. "I'm going to pick Daniel up at the church, run to the grocery store and then we'll stop at the park for a while."

A typical way to spend her time off from work. They lived in the upper level of an older home owned by their landlady, Mrs. Enderby. The retired schoolteacher lived on the first floor and had converted the tiny yard into a patchwork of flowers and shrubs. When Miranda had answered the ad in the newspaper, Mrs. Enderby had told her in no uncertain terms that, although she *liked* children, she didn't like them stomping around in her gardens.

The elderly woman also owned something Daniel referred to as a "scolding broom." It had appeared the first week they'd moved in upstairs. If Daniel got too close to a fascinating garden statue or one of the birdbaths, Mrs. Enderby came outside and shook her broom at him. Miranda didn't want to do anything to earn the woman's disapproval, so she took Daniel to Winchester Park to play. A lot.

"Since you're picking up Daniel today, will you do me a favor? I baked cookies for snack time tomorrow.

Naomi is expecting them so all you have to do is drop them off in the church kitchen."

"Sure." Miranda hadn't planned to go *inside* the church but it was a rare opportunity to actually be able to help Sandra out.

"Go ahead and scoot out of here now." Sandra smiled. "Darcy and Nina are coming in for the noon rush. Enjoy your afternoon with Daniel."

Miranda wasn't going to argue. The sun had burned its way through the clouds earlier that morning, promising a beautiful summer day. She didn't want to waste a minute of it.

She stopped at home first to shower, and then changed into denim capris and an eyelet top in a soft shade of yellow. She started to confine her hair into its usual twist but decided on a whim to leave it down. She thumbed through the dismal contents of her purse, thankful that lunch was included in the daily schedule at Sonshine Camp, and drove to the church.

Even if Chestnut Grove Community Church wasn't a historic landmark, Miranda would still have appreciated the sparkling red-and-white brick building with its arched windows and stained-glass inserts. A tall spire pierced the sky and the bell tower had been restored. Every day at noon, a joyous tune rolled into the air. The growing congregation had wisely resisted the urge to add on to the existing structure, preserving the building's simple elegance.

Miranda bypassed the parking lot near the church and drove around to the back. The youth center had been built next to the church itself and also housed the large fellowship hall. She had to drive around twice before finding a parking spot. She pushed her nervousness aside as she stepped into the spacious foyer.

The first person she saw was Naomi Fraser, Reverend Fraser's wife, apparently dressed like a character from the Bible in a long blue robe. The headpiece, fashioned from a dark blue bath towel, couldn't quite tame the bright red curls peeking out from the edges. When she saw Miranda, she gave her a friendly smile.

"Hello, Miranda. I'm afraid it's been one of those days." She laughed. "You heard of Little Bo Peep losing her sheep? Well, one of the shepherds lost one this morning. Caleb finally found it outside the youth wing, eating pizza crusts next to the Dumpster."

Miranda blinked. "A *real* sheep?"

"Oh, to be sure," Naomi said cheerfully. "We don't do anything halfway at Sonshine Camp. If the Bible story calls for a sheep, someone provides a sheep. Anyway, because of the excitement, we're running a little bit behind schedule now."

"I'm looking for my son, Daniel." Right after she said the words, she silently chided herself. With all the children who attended Chestnut Grove Community, Naomi wouldn't recognize the name of one little boy. Especially a boy she didn't see regularly.

"Sweet brown eyes. Green backpack, right? He's with the rest of the first graders at the park. The leaders took the children over there for games this morning to enjoy the beautiful weather. You can wait here for them to come back or go over there and pick him up."

"I'll go get him." Miranda quickly transferred the box of cookies to Naomi. "These are from Sandra."

"Tell her I said thank you." Naomi shifted the box under her arm, reached in and took out a jumbo chocolate-chip cookie. And took a large bite out of it.

Miranda stared.

"I have to make sure they taste good, don't I?" Naomi winked at her.

Miranda murmured a reply and made her escape. The last thing she wanted to do was stay at the church with Naomi. The woman reminded her of Sandra. Warm. Caring. And way too discerning.

When she drove to the park, she saw a cluster of children gathered in the sandlot, involved in a lively game of baseball. She shaded her eyes with her hand, looking for Daniel. If she knew her son, he'd be scoping out bugs or finding a cool rock to add to his collection. There was probably a leader assigned to the boys who didn't want to play baseball....

"Mom! Over here!"

Daniel's voice caught her attention and she followed it to its source.

Daniel was standing at home plate, his hands grasping a baseball bat.

Andrew Noble stood beside him.

Andrew almost didn't recognize Miranda.

Her hair was loose, falling past her shoulders and curling slightly at the ends. The faded denim pants she wore ended just below her knees and sun-kissed skin took over from there.

"There's my mom." Daniel beamed up at him.

Andrew grunted. It was the only sound he could make, given the fact his jaw scraped against home plate.

She looked beautiful. And unhappy.

He wasn't sure if it was because *he* was there or because Daniel was covered in dirt from his exuberant slide into second base during the first inning. Maybe both.

"Daniel…it's time to go." She glared at him.

Yeah, it was both.

Daniel's shoulders slumped. "But it's my turn to bat. And then we're having ice cream."

"We're almost finished." Wisdom told Andrew he probably shouldn't butt in. Sympathy for Daniel told Andrew he was already in trouble, so what did he have to lose? He rubbed his knuckles against the top of Daniel's head. "This guy has to get Ernest home."

On cue, Ernest waved from his spot on third.

Miranda wavered. "I suppose."

"Yes!" Daniel gave Andrew a high five. Now that he had his mom's blessing, he could focus on the game again. "Is this right, Andrew?"

"Mr. Noble," Miranda corrected under her breath.

Andrew's lips twitched. "You can wait in the dugout, Mom," he told her. "This shouldn't take long. Daniel's a natural."

Miranda pivoted sharply and walked toward the other adult leaders, who welcomed her into the shade of the dugout.

"Put your hands here, remember?" Andrew corrected Daniel's grip on the bat and stepped away. "Keep your eye on the ball, not the bat."

The pitcher growled and sent one flying.

Andrew held his breath and couldn't help offering up a silent prayer.

Crack.

He heard someone whoop with excitement. Out of the corner of his eye, he saw Miranda jumping up and down.

"Go, Daniel, go!" Andrew jumped to the side as Daniel flung the bat and took off running.

The ball soared over the pitcher's head and arched between two boys in the outfield. Ernest, who had shown his flair for the dramatic earlier in the game, pretended to run to home plate in slow motion.

Daniel ended up safe on third.

"That's it for the day, guys," Caleb Williams called. "Grab an ice-cream bar and we'll head back to church."

The chorus of protests subsided quickly at the words *ice-cream bar* and both teams charged toward the volunteers stationed by the cooler.

"Did you see me, Mom?" Daniel sprinted over to Miranda, his eyes shining with excitement.

"You did great. I didn't know you could hit a ball like that." Miranda ruffled his hair.

"Great game, Daniel." Caleb Williams jogged past them, collecting the sports equipment scattered around the field. "And thanks for filling in for Ben today, Andrew. I appreciate it."

"No problem." Andrew meant it. When Caleb had sent out an e-mail asking for an emergency replacement for Ben Cavanaugh, Andrew had called Zoe and asked her to reschedule his morning meetings. After talking to Rachel the night before, he had a strong hunch why Ben had taken the day off from his commitments.

When Andrew had arrived, he'd been surprised and pleased to have Daniel assigned to his group. Daniel had shadowed him most of the morning and it hadn't taken Andrew long to figure out why. Quiet and thoughtful, Daniel was a bit of an oddity to the other boys. He shied away from their rough and tumble antics, clearly uncomfortable being thrown into the competitions the rest of the boys thrived on. This made him a natural target for teasing, so he'd withdrawn, hanging on the sidelines most of the morning.

Until they'd chosen teams for baseball. Daniel had looked miserable and Andrew had guessed it was because he'd had his fill of being teased. When he'd discreetly taken Daniel to the side to tell him he didn't have to play, he'd inadvertently discovered the boy's misery wasn't because he didn't want to play, but because he *did.*

Andrew had encouraged him to join in, squelching the protests from the "red" team, who'd obviously considered him a liability. The protests had faded when Daniel had caught a fly ball in the outfield in the first ten minutes of the game.

"Can we stay and practice a little longer, Mom? Andrew said he'd pitch a couple to me."

Andrew saw the indecision on Miranda's face and the hopeful expression on Daniel's. He decided to put his neck in the noose once again. In the name of male bonding. "Hey, buddy. You better grab your ice-cream bar before they run out."

Daniel grinned and scooted off.

Leaving him and Miranda alone.

She stared at him, her expression guarded. And slightly accusing.

"He's good, Miranda," Andrew told her. "There's some natural talent there."

"He doesn't like to play baseball," Miranda murmured, confused. "He likes to collect the cards but he's never shown any interest in playing."

Andrew exhaled. "Maybe he hasn't been… encouraged."

His attempt at tact failed miserably. The gold sparks in Miranda's eyes came to life. And he was directly in the line of fire.

"Are you implying *I've* discouraged him?"

Tread carefully here, Andrew. You want to get to know the lady better. Criticizing her parenting skills probably isn't the way to her heart….

"Daniel told me he's always wanted to play but he can't because he likes science."

"What does that have to do with anything?"

"That was my question. According to Daniel, the kids in his class call him a brainiac. Somehow he got the impression he wouldn't be good at sports because he's good at academics. Someone even suggested that it doesn't matter if he's smaller than the other boys because it's more important for a person to exercise his brain than his biceps."

Miranda sat down hard on the bench and crossed her arms. A combination of guilt and defiance clouded her eyes. "That's true."

"You were the one who told him that?" The words were out before he could stop them.

"He is a little smaller than other boys. I didn't want him to get…hurt."

Andrew sat down next to her. She stiffened but didn't move away. He called that progress. Which was a shame, because what he was about to tell her had the potential to determine whether or not she'd ever speak to him again.

"Boys that age are held together by spit and sheer determination, Miranda. They're going to get bumped and scraped." He remembered the first time he'd met Daniel—wearing his X-ray "goggles" and makeshift cape—and wondered if she knew Daniel pretended to be a superhero. Someone brave. Unstoppable.

She shot him a look. "Spoken like a single man who isn't responsible for a child."

The faces of a hundred children suddenly materialized. Some laughing. Some crying. Every one of their images clear—and real—stored in his memory like pictures in an album.

How would she respond if you told her you do understand?

That he was even tempted to tell her about his life—the life lived apart from the man everyone thought he was—stunned him. He didn't know anything about her and for a moment he'd been tempted to spill information that could shut down a persona he'd spent years creating.

"I just don't want to see Daniel shortchanged," he said slowly. "Yes, he's a bright kid, but there are other things he might be good at. Things that could build up his confidence, too."

"Mom, there were some extra ones." Daniel rushed up to them, momentarily saving Andrew from the backlash he probably deserved. "Here's one for you, too, Andrew."

They both pasted on fake smiles and accepted the treats.

"So can we stay for a while, Mom? It's your day off, right?"

"I'm sure Mr. Noble is busy, Daniel."

Daniel gave him a pleading look.

"I took the afternoon off, too." Which was the truth. He just hadn't mentioned it to Zoe. Yet.

"Pastor Williams took all the baseball equipment," Miranda pointed out. "We don't have a bat and ball."

"Ah…I think I have one in the trunk of my car."

"You have a baseball bat and a ball in the trunk of your Ferrari?" Miranda stared him down.

He didn't mention he'd driven the Porsche to the church that morning. Or that he kept a box of stuffed bears in the trunk of his car, too. They came in handy when the kids he helped locate needed something to hold after their ordeal.

"You never know when the urge to play baseball is going to…ah, hit." *Go on. Tell me I'm not only a useless excuse of a man but a useless excuse of a man with an underdeveloped sense of humor….*

"That was terrible." She tilted her head and studied him.

Then she laughed. A low, husky laugh that melted away her reserve. And went straight to his toes.

Daniel looked back and forth between them, a wide grin on his face. For him, his mom's laugh settled it. "Mom, you can be the catcher. Andrew can pitch."

"It looks like I'm outnumbered." Miranda sighed now. "Let's play ball."

Chapter Seven

"Come on, Mom. *Run!*"

Lungs about to burst, Miranda clipped third base and headed for home. The only thing standing between her and victory was a six-foot-tall rock wall. With hazel eyes.

You're going to regret this tomorrow.

The drafts of oxygen she sucked in drowned out the voice of reason. Andrew loped closer, baseball in hand and a triumphant smile on his face.

She dropped. And slid.

Sand funneled into her shoes and dust clogged her nose.

When she opened her eyes, Daniel and Andrew stood over her, identical expressions of shock on their faces.

"Wow," Daniel breathed.

"What," Andrew said succinctly, "were you trying to do?"

"I had no choice." She managed a crooked smile.

Andrew didn't look convinced but he stretched out

his hand and pulled her to her feet. "I think we can safely call the game a tie. Is anyone interested in a burger? Or pizza?"

On her feet once again, Miranda stepped away. Andrew released her but for some strange reason, she could still feel his touch.

Why did Andrew Noble—Mr. Gorgeous and Out of My League, as Darcy had called him—awaken something in her she thought had died a long time ago? Several men had made their interest known since she'd come to Chestnut Grove but she'd successfully discouraged their attention. Flattery and friendly smiles didn't move her anymore.

And neither did men who tried to use her son to get to her, she reminded herself.

"We can't." She brushed at the dirt that caked the fabric of her capris so she wouldn't have to look at him. It wasn't fair. He was disheveled and still looked terrific while she resembled a human dust cloud. "Daniel and I have some errands to run."

And she wasn't exactly dressed for lunch out even if the dress code called for casual. She could only imagine what people would think if they saw her and Andrew together. Maybe that she was the Noble Foundation's latest charity case?

Daniel looked disappointed but Miranda refused to budge. She'd already spent an hour in the company of a man she had nothing in common with. A man her son was already becoming too attached to.

"I can have something delivered."

"To the park?" Daniel's eyes widened.

"Why not?" Andrew smiled at her over Daniel's head but Miranda didn't smile back.

Of course he could. He was Andrew Noble. He could probably make a phone call and fly in a chef from Paris. Burgers in Winchester Park were the equivalent of the snap of his fingers.

And what would he expect in return for his benevolence? Did he assume someone like her would be thrilled to have his attention? However short-lived?

"It's just lunch, Miranda."

She'd thought she'd become adept at hiding her emotions. Hal had taken a twisted pleasure in his ability to play with them, so she'd learned to keep her feelings to herself. Andrew's quiet words told her she hadn't mastered that harsh lesson as well as she'd thought she had.

Andrew took her silence as a yes.

Miranda might consider herself to be aloof but she didn't have a clue her eyes reflected every thought and feeling.

She didn't trust him.

Not that he blamed her. He'd spent years letting everyone believe he was the kind of man a woman like Miranda couldn't trust. Especially if she'd been hurt before.

There'd been a time in his life he'd naively believed his family background wouldn't matter. That having the last name Noble wouldn't be a liability to the man God called him to be.

People hadn't paid much attention to him as a teenager. In private school, he'd flown under the media's radar. That had changed when he'd turned eighteen and received his full inheritance. All it had taken was one photographer from a popular magazine to snap a photo of him on the deck of a friend's sailboat and declare that "Andrew Noble's trust fund is free…and so is he."

He'd ignored it and gone on with his life. The next week, the same photographer had been waiting outside the little church he'd worshipped at every Sunday. The photo that had appeared in the newspaper had been strategically placed next to one of a popular club, filled with a drunken bunch of his former classmates. He hadn't been there but it hadn't seemed to matter.

Andrew Noble Goes to Church on Sunday to Make up for Wild Party on Saturday.

That was when he'd realized the dream he'd been praying about and fine tuning would be jeopardized simply because of his last name. Anything he was involved in would become fodder for the gossip columns.

Even his faith.

As a child, his abduction by a family employee had been a defining moment. He'd been too young to put into words what had happened during those four days of terror, but he knew his prayers had brought the God of the Universe into that basement prison to comfort him.

By the time he'd inherited his trust fund, he knew God was calling him to do something a little risky. Something that would give innocent kids hope—the same hope he'd been given.

If it meant he had to let people think he lived a life of no purpose to protect that calling, it was worth it. The *kids* were worth it. He didn't have to prove himself to anyone, but he did have to be faithful to what God called him to do.

He'd felt the cost of that decision over the years but he'd never been as burdened by it as he was now. The expression of mistrust on Miranda's face said it all. She'd let her guard down and had fun. And now she regretted it. He could see the conflict in her eyes. She wondered if he expected something in return for something as simple as pizza.

He blew out a silent breath, knowing he should let her go. But Miranda looked as if she could use a friend. So did Daniel. And Daniel didn't care who he was; all he knew was that Andrew understood about baseball and superheroes and what it was like to be afraid.

He made a decision. Right or wrong, they were stuck with him for the rest of the afternoon. Before Miranda could change her mind about lunch in the park, he slipped his cell phone out of his pocket and made a call.

"Pizza or burgers?" he whispered to Daniel.

"Pizza."

"Pepperoni or frog legs?"

Daniel burst out laughing. "Frog legs."

Miranda grimaced.

"Mushrooms? Green peppers?" He arched an eyebrow at her.

She rolled her eyes. And smiled. The smile he wanted to see a lot more of. "I'm not picky."

"Oh, really?" Andrew frowned into the phone and shook his head at Daniel. "No frog legs today, bud. Does pepperoni work for you?"

Daniel nodded vigorously.

He topped the order off with sodas and bread sticks and then snapped the phone shut. "Half an hour."

"Let's play some more baseball."

Andrew glanced at Miranda. He wondered if she knew how adorably rumpled she looked with her windblown hair and flushed cheeks.

"I think we should find some shade for your mom."

"That sounds wonderful." Miranda's heartfelt sigh squashed any argument Daniel might have raised.

That Daniel and his mother shared a close bond was evident in the way he slipped his hand into hers and cheerfully began to recite the highlights of another morning at Sonshine Camp. Andrew trailed along behind them, enjoying the sound of Daniel's chatter and the sparkle in his eyes.

"...and Andrew likes my name. It's just like the man in the story Mrs. Fraser read to us."

"Daniel and the lion's den," Miranda murmured.

"It's Andrew's favorite story, isn't it, Andrew?" He looked at him for affirmation and grinned when Andrew nodded. "God closed the mouths of the lions so they didn't bite Daniel. They could have, Mom, but Mrs. Fraser says they were like big kittens and Daniel probably used them as pillows."

Miranda's silence and the sudden tension in her shoulders carved a hollow in the pit of Andrew's stomach. He'd assumed that because Daniel was attending Sonshine Camp, he and Miranda worshipped at Chestnut Grove Community.

Now he wasn't so sure.

"Can you imagine that?" There was an awestruck look on Daniel's face. "Sleeping on *lions?*"

Miranda forced a smile. "It's a nice story."

Their eyes met and Andrew saw a mixture of cynicism and weary acceptance in hers.

It's a nice story. If it were true.

Daniel's chatter filled the awkward silence that fell between them as he clamored onto the bench of the picnic table.

Fortunately, it wasn't long before a black SUV pulled up next to them.

A young woman hopped out, a scrap of pink silk tucked in the pocket of the tuxedo jacket she wore. With a wide smile, she snapped a linen tablecloth over the picnic table and put a white pillar candle in the center, which she lit with a dramatic flourish.

Daniel watched in fascination as she set out a pizza the size of his bicycle tire, a crystal pitcher of soda and a basket of breadsticks.

"Enjoy. I'll be back to pick up everything later." And she bounced back into her vehicle and drove away.

"Did you order all this?" Gingerly, Miranda picked up one of the heavy linen napkins.

Was this a trick question? Because she'd been standing two feet away while he'd placed the order. Then he realized what she meant.

"Gabriella owns the pizzeria. She's rather...dramatic."

He should have known Gabriella would assume his order for an impromptu lunch in the park would mean he was with a woman, so she'd pulled out all the stops to help him charm his "date."

It wasn't Gabriella's fault this was Miranda Jones, who was less than charmed as she stared at the transformation of the humble picnic table. She didn't say it out loud but he knew what she was thinking. That he was spoiled. That all he had to do was crook his finger and people jumped to do his bidding.

Even Daniel suddenly seemed subdued.

Andrew suppressed a sigh and decided there was nothing he could do about it now except to make a mental note that, next time he ordered takeout from Gabriella's, he'd tell her to throw the pizza in the cardboard box and leave it at that.

"Do you mind if I ask a blessing for the food?"

Miranda hesitated for a split second and then shook her head. Daniel folded his hands on the table and pinched his eyes shut.

"Lord..." Andrew knew this wasn't the time to pour out all the things in his heart that hammered to get out. Such as his confusing attraction to Miranda. The reality that she wasn't a believer. The protective feelings he had for her and Daniel. He'd better keep it simple and uncomplicated. Although he had the feeling that *uncomplicated* wasn't going to describe his feelings. "Thank you for the food you've provided and the beautiful day you've given us to enjoy. Thank you for Miranda. And Daniel—"

"And for baseball," Daniel chimed in.

Miranda gasped and Andrew chuckled.

"And thank you for baseball," he added solemnly. "Amen."

Andrew opened his eyes and found Miranda watching him. For an instant, he saw the questions flicker in her expressive eyes. Was his prayer sincere? And if it was, how did it connect with the man she'd read about in the newspapers?

I have just as many questions about you, Andrew thought. *Maybe this afternoon we'll find some answers to them...*

He poured a glass of lemonade and handed it to her.

"Thank you." Her voice barely broke above a whisper.

She gave Daniel a slice of pizza and added a bread stick to his plate, then handed him a fork.

Andrew's eyebrow rose and Miranda's cheeks took on a fetching peach hue.

"It's messy." She waggled the fork at him.

"Pizza is supposed to be messy, not dainty." Deliberately, he picked up a piece of pizza and took a bite, then winked at Daniel.

Daniel imitated him, right down to the mischievous wink he gave his mother.

The responding humor in her eyes and the subtle tilt of her lips said she'd given in. At least on the matter of fingers versus forks.

Miranda was definitely a contradiction. Wary one minute, warm the next. Somehow, he sensed that her reserve wasn't a natural part of her personality. It was something she held in place like a shield and he'd been fortunate to glimpse the real Miranda Jones when the shield had momentarily fallen away. Like during their impromptu baseball game.

He wanted to know what made her tick. Just when he wondered how he could stretch out the day to spend more time with them, his cell phone rang. The only ring tone he couldn't ignore.

Andrew stifled a groan.

"I have to take this." He didn't wait for Miranda to respond and he could feel the weight of two pairs of eyes on him as he strode toward the pond, out of earshot.

"Are you available?" The voice on the other end of the phone was soft and smoky. With a core of steel.

Genevieve. The voice and the name conjured up hot southern nights and bluesy jazz. The fact that both belonged to a petite, silver-haired grandmother should have brought a smile to his face. And it might have, except the only time Genevieve called him was when a child was missing.

He looked toward the picnic table. Miranda had stopped eating. Daniel was plowing through another slice of pizza with the exuberance only a growing boy could display.

Just when he'd been trying to convince her there was more to him than Andrew the Irresponsible, leaving her and Daniel in the middle of lunch—with no excuse—was going to prove to her that there wasn't.

And he couldn't tell her the truth.

"Of course I'm available."

Miranda couldn't sleep.

The air conditioner in the bedroom window had sputtered and died just after midnight and the muscles in her legs were still protesting the unscheduled baseball game she'd been coerced into playing that afternoon.

She tried to convince herself that those were the reasons she was staring at the ceiling at two o'clock in the morning. But she knew better. What kept her awake was Andrew. Just about the time she'd started to think there might be more to him than fast cars and trips to Europe on a private jet he'd proved there wasn't.

She rolled over restlessly, hugging the pillow against her chest.

"Is Andrew mad at me, Mom?"

Daniel's words still tugged at her heart.

When Andrew had walked back to the picnic table, she'd known he was going to leave. She'd known it even before his lips had curved into that heartbreaking smile and he'd offered a casual shrug and told them simply that something "had come up."

Miranda wanted to be angry. She should still be angry. It would protect her from falling for Andrew's roguish charm in the future. And she might have been successful if not for one thing. Regret. She'd seen it in his eyes—for just a moment—before he'd sauntered toward the parking lot.

She tried to convince herself she'd imagined that brief, raw flash in his eyes that had appealed to her to understand.

To understand what? That whatever or whoever had called him away was more important than a little boy's disappointment?

Or yours?

Miranda tossed the question away as quickly as she did the cotton sheet draped over her legs. The darkness and the heat were stifling. She gave up on sleeping and padded down the hall to check on Daniel.

Unlike her, he was sound asleep, his arm curled around Lily, the stuffed frog she'd given to him on his third birthday. She remembered with a smile how her little boy had carried the frog everywhere for a couple of years. Now, worn and well loved, it remained his bedtime companion, waiting faithfully on his pillow until the nightly tuck-in ritual they shared.

She picked up the edge of the sheet he'd kicked off and noticed his pajama bottoms landed several inches above his ankle. Once again she was faced with the bittersweet reality that Daniel was growing up.

She couldn't believe how swiftly Daniel had attached himself to Andrew. Or that he'd confided in him. All this time she'd thought Daniel had no interest in playing sports, never realizing his classmates had slapped a label on him because of his studious nature.

She shared the blame. When Daniel had shown no interest in sports, she hadn't encouraged him. She'd told Andrew the truth about not wanting him to get hurt.

Hal's unpredictable nature had made her even more protective than most first-time parents. Especially because Hal had used Daniel as a threat to keep her in the relationship. Shortly after she'd broken up with him, she'd come home from work to find him sitting in her kitchen. He'd been in the apartment long enough to make dinner. What had terrified her the most wasn't that he'd had a key made without her knowledge, but the fact that when she'd told him she had to go pick up Daniel from the babysitter's, he'd smugly told her that he already had. She'd rushed into Daniel's bedroom and found him sleeping peacefully.

Hal had loomed in the doorway, watching as she'd gathered Daniel into her arms.

"I can find him, Miranda. I can always find him. And then I'll find you," he'd said with chilling matter-of-factness.

Two nights later, she'd taken Daniel and left Atlanta.

Hal's threat cast a shadow over her life that had never been lifted. There were two suitcases in the closet—packed and waiting—in case he found them again.

At least the nightmare Hal had put her through had taught her something. It was up to her to protect her son.

Chapter Eight

"I guess we know why Mr. Tall, Dark and Restless hasn't been here all week." Darcy slapped the latest issue of the *Gazette* down on the counter.

Miranda didn't need to look down to know what Darcy was pointing to. She'd already seen it. A photo of Andrew Noble, his arm casually draped around the shoulders of a well-known singer. A *beautiful* well-known singer.

"Did you check on table three?" Miranda ignored the unexpected stab of pain as she pushed the newspaper away and caught a glimpse of Andrew's handsome face. According to the caption, the photo had been taken in Nashville the day after he'd left her and Daniel in the park.

"They're fine. Picky about the way their eggs are cooked, but fine." Darcy wasn't going to be distracted as she picked up the newspaper and gave it a dramatic shake. "Tell me why men always go for shallow and beautiful instead of deep thinkers."

Miranda, who happened to know the T-shirt Darcy wore under her uniform featured a bright transfer of a popular breakfast cereal, tried not to smile.

"Just because she's beautiful doesn't mean she's shallow," Miranda felt the need to point out. In the interest of being fair.

"Beautiful women are shallow because they *can* be," Darcy argued. "There's no *pressure* to have a nice personality—"

"Are you only giving your opinion today, Darcy, or are you giving refills on coffee, too?" A man sitting at a nearby table raised his coffee cup.

Darcy rolled her eyes. "Coming right up, Mr. Brewster. Did you know coffee isn't good for people? Studies show it makes them *cranky.*"

"That's only if a person doesn't get any. It's called *caffeine withdrawal.* Want me to tell you the symptoms?"

As Darcy and Mr. Brewster continued their banter, Miranda shoved the newspaper under the counter.

Was the woman in the picture the reason he'd left so abruptly that day?

She hadn't seen Andrew since their picnic in the park and tried to convince herself it didn't matter. She didn't want him coming to the diner. She didn't want to deal with Daniel's hero worship of the man or the strange, mixed-up emotions he stirred inside her.

Andrew was exactly the way the newspapers described him. The picture proved it. He lived in the moment. He only stuck with something until a better model came along. A single mother who waited on tables and a seven-year-old boy hadn't kept his interest for more than an hour.

"You can't believe everything you read." Sandra scooted around the counter and tapped the numbers on the old-fashioned cash register.

The woman had eyes in the back of her head. But in this instance, Miranda knew Sandra was wrong.

"Seeing is believing, Sandra."

"Sometimes our eyes trick us into believing what we *want* to see."

Miranda couldn't argue with that. Hal had swept into her life with hurricane force. His magnetic charm and good looks had initially blinded her from seeing his true self. She'd ignored the warning signs. And she wasn't going to make the same mistake again.

"Uh-oh. Here comes trouble," Darcy sang out. "Make that *double* trouble."

Daniel and Olivia Cavanaugh burst into the diner, dodging several customers who were on their way out the door. Leah followed in their wake; baby Joseph sleeping peacefully against her heart in a baby sling fashioned from a length of eye-catching purple batik. It was a colorful contrast to the vintage-style lavender dress she wore.

"Hi, Mom," Daniel panted. "Mrs. Cavanaugh wants to talk to you."

"I promised Naomi I would hand deliver this, Miranda." Leah pulled a bright yellow flyer from the crocheted bag slung over her other shoulder. "The final program for camp is tonight and all the parents are invited. The volunteers are recognized and the children sing a few of the songs they learned during the week and put on a short skit."

"And cookies." Olivia scrambled onto one of the

stools and pushed off the floor with her pink sandaled foot, sending it into a slow spin.

"And cookies." Leah smiled at her irrepressible daughter.

Miranda glanced down at the flyer in her hands instead of the hopeful look in Daniel's eyes.

"I'm going to finish my birdhouse tomorrow but the paint won't be dry until after the program. Then I can bring it home." Daniel offered another reason to attend the program.

Which, Miranda acknowledged ruefully, tipped the scale in his favor. Lately, there'd been three topics of discussion at mealtime—baseball, the birdhouse he was building during craft-time…and Andrew Noble.

"We better not miss it, then." Miranda wrapped her arms around him in a fierce hug and Daniel giggled.

"We can sit together if you'd like," Leah offered. "Daniel and Olivia will be part of the program. I'll be in the back row in case this one starts to fuss," she said gesturing to the sleeping baby in the sling.

At the moment, with his golden-brown eyelashes fanning his pudgy cheeks and his bow-shaped mouth pursed in sleep, Joseph Cavanaugh didn't look as if he had a fussy bone in his body. But if Miranda had to go to church, the back row sounded like the perfect place to be.

"I think I'll take you up on that."

"Great. Six-thirty. We'll see you there." Leah took hold of Olivia's hand as she jumped down.

"How is Ben doing?" Sandra asked, her voice full of compassion.

The baby stirred in Leah's arms, as if sensing his

mother's sudden change in moods. "He's been talking to Reverend Fraser the past few days...and praying a lot. We all have. He hasn't called the Watsons yet, but he's close."

"It's a hard thing—stepping back into the past. But sometimes it's the only way we can move into the future." Sandra sighed. "Knowing I could trust God and that He was with me was the only thing that gave me hope when I was searching for Kelly."

The look of complete understanding the two women exchanged—born from the faith that connected them—made Miranda feel like an outsider again. She knew Sandra and Leah had both been through difficult situations. Why had their faith flourished during the heat of their trials while hers had withered and died?

It was another reason she felt inadequate. Flawed somehow.

Sandra gave Leah a bracing hug, stirring the air with the scent of vanilla and cinnamon. "You tell Ben that Sandra's praying, too, sugar."

"I will," Leah promised as she shepherded Olivia toward the door.

"I can hear Isaac talking to himself in the kitchen. I better see what the problem is." Sandra blew Daniel a kiss. "I'll be right back with your lunch, young man."

Daniel imitated Olivia's spin on the stool. "Mom? Do you think Andrew will be at the program?"

Miranda's heart skipped a beat. She hadn't even considered the possibility. As far as she knew, he'd only volunteered one morning.

"I don't think so, Daniel. I'm sure he's got better things to do."

Just like he had better things to do the day he had lunch delivered to the park.

Disappointment clouded Daniel's face. "I wanted to tell him that Pastor Caleb let me pitch today and I struck out Cam Butterfield."

"What's wrong with telling your mom you struck out Cam Butterfield? I happen to be your number-one fan, Mr. Jones." She picked up a fluffy dish towel and shook it like a pompom.

Daniel giggled and the sound went straight to Miranda's heart. "You're weird sometimes, Mom."

"Right back at you." She dabbed the corner of the towel playfully against his nose, relieved he'd forgotten about Andrew Noble.

"Mom? Will you tell Andrew about Cam Butterfield if you see him?"

Or not.

"Daniel..." She had to do it. For Daniel's sake. And maybe for her own. "Mr. Noble is a busy man. Remember how he left us in the park—"

"He had to, Mom." Daniel's eyes were wide. "He got the call."

"The call?"

"He had to help someone."

"Did he tell you that?" Miranda couldn't remember Andrew saying anything to Daniel that afternoon other than goodbye.

"No."

"I have no idea what you're talking about," Miranda said patiently. "If An—*Mr. Noble*—didn't tell you he had to help someone, what makes you think he did?"

"I just know."

To Miranda's astonishment, Daniel's eyes filled with tears.

Instinctively, she reached out and squeezed his hand. "Daniel, we don't know anything about Mr. Noble. Sometimes we like someone and it makes us believe things about them that might not be true."

"I know he's one of them, Mom. He *told* me that day he fixed my bicycle."

It was official. She needed to find a manual that would help her navigate the uncharted territory of a seven-year-old boy's mind. "One of *who?*"

Daniel looked up at her earnestly. "One of the *good* guys."

Oh, Daniel.

Miranda closed her eyes briefly against the crushing weight of regret that slammed against her heart. She didn't want to be the one to contradict Daniel's staunch belief in a man he barely knew. But the proof was there in Andrew's lifestyle.

"We'll talk about this later," she said softly.

Even though everything inside her screamed that she couldn't trust her instincts anymore when it came to men, the startling truth was realizing she was just like Daniel. There was something about Andrew Noble that made her want to believe in him.

She wanted to believe he was one of the good guys, too.

"Welcome back, stranger. I'm going to run out of pages in my scrapbook if your picture keeps turning up in the newspaper," Rachel teased from her cozy nest on the sofa.

Great. Andrew slumped into the tweed recliner and plowed his fingers through his hair, not sure he wanted to see the article she'd referred to. He'd gotten so used to flashbulbs going off in his face when he walked out the door, he barely noticed them anymore. But now, because of Miranda, he was acutely aware that every article and every photo had become a potential roadblock to getting to know her better.

"I'm sorry I bailed on the Foundation for a few days," he said. Call it denial, but he could wait to see whatever he'd done that had made the headlines. The adrenaline he'd lived on for the past forty-eight hours was wearing off, leaving him vulnerable to the fatigue chewing on the edges of his brain.

"Tell me why?" Rachel asked brightly.

"Sorry. No can do." Lack of trust wasn't the reason he hadn't told his family about his work as Guardian—it was to protect them. It hurt a little that the people closest to him believed the same things the avid readers of the society pages did, but it was necessary.

Rachel gave a very un-Noble-like snort and handed him the newspaper. "Fine. I can accept that your life is shrouded in mystery, but please tell me *she* wasn't the reason why you left your post at the Foundation."

He took one look at the newspaper clipping and crumpled it like an empty paper cup. It was worse than he'd thought.

Rachel blinked. "Wow."

Dark color rushed up his neck and into his face. "Sorry. Did you want that?"

"Not anymore." She flicked a curious glance at the wad of paper clenched in his fist.

"How does something that happened in Nashville, Tennessee—" Andrew began to methodically shred the paper into narrow strips "—make the gossip column in Richmond, Virginia?"

"Ah, your dedication to recycling is inspiring." Rachel looked meaningfully at the former newspaper. "But I think the technical term is the *society page,* not gossip column. And it's not where it happened, it's *who* it happened to. You're news, Andrew."

Which meant Miranda had probably seen it.

Juliana Overstreet was a popular Christian singer whose father happened to be one of the retired private investigators Andrew worked with on occasion. Charles Overstreet specialized in Internet crime and because the fourteen-year-old girl who'd disappeared had spent hours chatting online, Andrew had immediately pulled him in to help.

Within hours, the teenager had been located in a nearby shopping mall with the suspect, whom they'd taken into custody. Because it had been late in the evening by the time local law enforcement had wrapped things up, Andrew had taken Charles up on his invitation to have dinner with him and Juliana.

This wasn't the first time the newspapers had linked Andrew and Juliana romantically, but she was happily engaged to one of the musicians in her band. She had become a good friend over the years and she'd listened patiently while Andrew had spent most of the evening talking about Miranda and Daniel. As they'd left the restaurant, a photographer had stepped in front of them and snapped their picture.

He'd assumed the photographer's interest was Juliana, never dreaming the photo would be reprinted in the *Richmond Gazette.*

Frustration surged through him. "It was dinner. With a *friend.* Not news."

"Do you want to talk about this?"

"No."

Rachel's lips twitched. "At the risk of pointing out the obvious, not many people have as many *friends* as you do."

He scowled. "Why don't the reporters torture you? We're from the same family."

"That's true, but I live a boring life compared to you. No private island. No yacht. I don't date European royalty." She yawned for effect. "I'm just a working girl. At least, I *was.*"

"I don't have a private island," he muttered.

"And I exchanged the name Noble for Cavanaugh. It's like wearing dark sunglasses and a wig."

"Right." Andrew rose to his feet and stalked toward the door.

"Where are you going? You just got here!"

"I'm hungry."

"You don't have to go out. People have been dropping off casseroles and salads all week," Rachel called, trying to lure him back.

He kept going.

"I suppose if Miranda Jones was here to bring it out, you'd stay."

Andrew stopped dead in his tracks. And slowly turned around. "What did you say?"

"You heard me." She covered the lower half of her face with a cashmere throw to hide her smirk.

He stared at her in disbelief. "How did… You have *spies.*"

She gave an indignant huff. "I have *friends.*"

"What else do you know?" His eyes narrowed.

Rachel shrugged. "I know enough to know that answering that question will get me in trouble. Now, shoo. Miranda gets off work in a few minutes. If you hurry, you might catch her."

He shot her a disgusted look and made for the door.

"I don't hear you denying it," she called after him.

He wasn't. It was probably the best piece of advice his cousin had ever given him.

But he wasn't about to admit it.

Chapter Nine

"Did you know he had the starring role in the skit?" Leah whispered.

Miranda shook her head, unable to take her eyes off Daniel, a tiny figure pacing the stage in a heavy terry-cloth bathrobe that dragged across the floor. An assortment of stuffed lions surrounded him.

"Daniel! Daniel! Was your God able to save you?" A little boy wearing a sequined crown rushed to the edge of the sheet-draped corner.

"My God saved me," Daniel called back. "Come and see!"

The "king" pretended to pull Daniel out of the lion's den and the boys embraced. Then, in an obvious ad-lib, they smacked their hands together in a high five.

Laughter rippled around the darkened room.

Miranda felt hot tears scald the back of her eyes as the other cast members scurried out, formed an uneven line and bowed. As the lights flickered on to signal the end of the program, Miranda barely heard Caleb Williams give a brief summary of the week and close the program with a stirring prayer.

She tried to convince herself the tears were because Daniel was part of the skit and not because of its message. She remembered seeing the fleeting disappointment in Andrew's eyes in the park that afternoon when she'd told him the biblical account of Daniel was a nice story. Even if there'd been a time when she'd believed God really did intervene—that He cared enough to stretch out His hand and rescue those who belonged to Him—she couldn't change the past. He hadn't saved Lorraine and Tom. He hadn't even saved her from Hal. How could she trust Him to rescue her in the future?

"Are you and Daniel staying for refreshments, Miranda?" Leah asked.

Miranda looked away so Leah wouldn't notice her tears. "I think so." She searched the crowd for a glimpse of Daniel. He was probably already in line with Olivia Cavanaugh for cookies and punch.

"Olivia and Daniel get along really well." Leah's words told Miranda their thoughts had taken the same path. "Joseph isn't quite old enough for her to boss around yet so I think she's using Daniel as practice."

"She's coaxed him out of his shell, that's true."

Leah laughed. "Coaxed. *Yanked.* However you want to look at it. I better get Joseph out of the nursery or he'll be raising the roof for his bedtime snack."

Miranda didn't know her way around the church very well so she followed the exodus of people out the door to the fellowship hall. Olivia was close to the front of the line but Daniel wasn't with her.

"Livy, do you know where Daniel is?"

Olivia shook her head. "He said he'd meet me here after he gave his costume back to Mrs. Fraser."

"I'll see if I can find—"

"He went with the man," the little boy standing in front of Olivia interrupted.

"What man?" Fear stripped away her voice, leaving it a hoarse whisper.

The boy shrugged. "I don't know him."

Miranda's knees felt weak but she pushed through the crowd on autopilot. Where was she supposed to start looking for him? One of the many rooms in the church? The parking lot?

Don't panic, Miranda, think.

She began to catalog what Daniel had been wearing. *Khaki shorts. A green T-shirt with a tree frog silk-screened on the front.*

"Daniel?" Her voice thinned as she walked through the crowd of people, calling his name.

Maybe Pastor Williams or one of the other male teachers who'd volunteered in his class during the week was with him, trying to find *her.*

She bumped into Anne and grabbed her arm like a lifeline.

"Have you seen Daniel?"

Anne shook her head. "No, but—"

Miranda didn't wait for her to elaborate. The rational side of her knew she'd find Daniel safe and sound but a dark cloud stained her thoughts.

I'll always find him, Miranda. And then I'll find you.

She stumbled up the stairs and blindly turned a corner. Sunday-school classrooms flanked both sides of the hall. Daniel had taken her into one of the rooms shortly after they'd arrived at church to show her the birdhouse he'd made. The lights were on but an eerie quiet had settled in that part of the building. The laughter and voices of the people in the fellowship hall had faded.

"Daniel?" Her voice cracked as she called his name again.

"I'm in here."

Miranda's knees went weak when she heard the familiar voice. Daniel, concentrating on wrapping the birdhouse in newspaper, barely looked up when she lurched into the room.

Relief and exasperation waged an internal battle. Relief won hands down. "Daniel Thomas Jones, where have you been?"

Daniel blinked. "Here."

Miranda sank into one of the small plastic chairs, her hand over her heart as she willed it into its natural rhythm again.

"What's the matter, Mom? Are you sick?" Daniel hurried over to her, his eyes huge.

"No. I was *worried.* Someone said you left with a…man."

"I did."

"What?" Miranda gulped the word. "Who?"

"Me."

Her knees turned to jelly. Again.

Andrew. Her mouth worked but no sound came out. He was the last person she expected to see.

"Hello, Miranda."

He looked tired. She was horrified by the sudden urge to brush her fingers against the rough stubble that shadowed his jaw and smooth a wayward strand of hair off his forehead.

"Andrew came to watch me in the play," Daniel said. "And look what he gave me." He picked up a leather baseball glove.

Miranda swallowed hard against the emotions that welled up inside and closed her throat. "Danny, I think Olivia is waiting for you downstairs. I'll finish wrapping up your birdhouse."

"Okay. Are you going to stay, Andrew?"

"I'm not sure yet, champ." He gave Miranda a speculative look.

"I'll save a cookie for you, Mom. Something chocolate." Daniel dashed out the door.

"Are you all right? You look pale." Two strides brought Andrew to her side. "Should I get Eli?"

"No." Miranda realized Andrew's presence was far from comforting. "It… I'm fine. Now."

He frowned. Miranda looked down but his hand cupped her chin and gently lifted it up. He searched her eyes, looking for the truth. "You couldn't find Daniel. Did you think something had happened to him? Here?"

The question made her fear seem irrational and silly. But she couldn't deny it. "Someone said they'd seen him leave with an adult. It's stupid, I know, but—"

"No, it's not." Andrew let out a slow breath. "It's my

fault. Daniel saw me talking to Pastor Fraser right after the program. He told me you were with Leah and he was so anxious to show me the birdhouse he'd made, I didn't stop to think about how you'd feel if you couldn't find him."

His willingness to accept he'd made a mistake chipped away at her defenses. Miranda tried to find a way to shore up the wall between them. "Daniel can't accept the baseball glove, Mr. Noble."

Andrew was motionless as he stared at some unknown point on the wall.

"Why?" The simple question broke the silence.

Miranda stood up and walked to the window, needing to put some space between them. It didn't help. "I don't know you."

"You don't know me," Andrew repeated the words. "Is that the real reason, Miranda? Or is it because you *think* you do?"

The photo of him and Juliana Overstreet flashed in her mind. And so did the memory of the unexpected hurt she'd felt when he'd left her and Daniel in the park with no explanation. Her frustration bubbled to the surface and spilled over.

"Daniel has always been quiet but he can't stop talking about you. He even came up with some crazy reason why you left us in the park. He said you got *the call* to help someone. He's been…disappointed before. Can't you see, it isn't good for him to get attached to you—to trust you? It's only going to lead to—" Her voice broke off when she realized the words were as true for herself as they were for Daniel. And judging from the expression on Andrew's face, he knew it, too.

"What is it going to lead to?" He moved toward her.

Miranda shook her head mutely and braced herself, anticipating he'd stand close enough to intimidate her with his size and strength. He didn't. He stopped several feet away and shoved his hands in his front pockets.

"I'm sorry I couldn't tell you why I left."

Miranda was confused by the way he phrased it. He wasn't sorry he'd left, but sorry he couldn't tell her why?

"Miranda? I'd never hurt Daniel. Do you believe me?"

She *wanted* to believe him. And that was what scared her the most.

"He thinks you're some kind of hero. He's going to be disappointed." *I'm going to be disappointed.*

"A hero? I guess I'll have to set him straight, won't I?" Andrew's lips twisted. "Please let Daniel keep the baseball glove. I didn't mean to overstep my boundaries." When she didn't respond, he walked toward the door. "He's a great kid. You're doing a good job, Miranda."

Out of all the things he could have said to end their conversation, it was the last thing she'd expected. And exactly what she needed to hear.

"Scoot down, girls. Another one of the belly buddies has arrived," Meg Kierney announced.

"I think we're going to need a bigger table, Miranda." Kelly Van Zandt eyed the group of friends who'd been waiting her arrival, one hand resting on her bulging tummy.

"I don't need a bigger table—" Pilar Fletcher sighed "—I need a bigger *chair.*"

"Oh, please." Kelly laughed as Anne and Leah maneuvered their chairs to make more room. "You're as slim as ever. From the back."

Pilar wrinkled her nose. "Pretty soon I won't be able to see my feet."

"Would you be more comfortable in a booth?" Miranda ventured.

"We're fine." Meg's bright auburn curls bounced in response to her decisive nod. "Life is crazy enough at the moment. Something has to stay the same. Like sitting at our favorite table."

A silence settled over the noisy group as everyone absorbed the truth in what she'd said. Miranda knew Meg was referring to the recent backlash in the community over the documents found hidden in the Harcourt mansion. The story had been leaked to the press and several scathing letters to the editor, directed at the Harcourt family, had already appeared in the weekend edition of the *Gazette*.

According to the letters Miranda had read, two families had already discovered their children's adoptions hadn't been legal. She'd lain awake the night before, battling the fear that Daniel's adoption might be one of the ones that came into question.

"Meg's right," Pilar said, her tone deliberately light. She patted her tummy. "The only thing that's changed today is my coffee preference. I'm ordering decaf."

Miranda took the rest of the drink orders and went behind the counter. By the time she returned with the tray, everyone was in line for the buffet except Anne.

"I had to call home and find out how Christina is doing," Anne confessed with a smile. "Not that I don't trust Caleb and Dylan with her, of course, but if she's not in my arms, I just feel like something's...missing."

"I know what you mean." Miranda relived the heart-stopping moment when she couldn't find Daniel. The panic she'd felt had melted away the instant she'd realized he'd been with Andrew. Did that mean on some level she trusted him?

Was that what Andrew had wanted to hear?

She shook the unsettling thought away.

"I'm glad Daniel came to Sonshine Camp," Anne continued. "He seems so shy but he actually volunteered to play the part of Daniel in the skit."

Miranda had been surprised, too, but not as surprised as she'd been when Daniel had shown her the plaque his teacher had given him for memorizing all his verses. It had to be a coincidence that the verse on the wooden plaque was the same one she hadn't been able to shake out of her thoughts all week.

See, I have engraved you on the palms of my hands.

"It was good for him," Miranda murmured.

"The youth group is helping out with games at the Fourth of July celebration this week. Caleb even mentioned forming some teams for baseball. Are you working?"

"Sandra closes the diner so everyone can have the day off."

Anne's blue eyes lit up. "You should join us. Reverend Fraser and Scott Crosby are manning the grills and everyone brings a dish to pass. We sit in the shade, eat way too much and then watch the fireworks."

"Speaking of eating too much," Meg said as she, Pilar and Leah rejoined Anne at the table. "It's not fair that I gain a pound just by *looking* at Sandra's homemade cinnamon rolls."

"Olivia will be at the celebration," Leah added, making no effort to hide the fact she'd overheard at least part of Miranda's conversation with Anne.

"I'm not sure what our plans are yet." Miranda thought of the suitcases stashed in the closet.

Kelly winced suddenly and pressed her fingers against her ribs. "I'm convinced Ross and I have a future ballerina in here."

"Or maybe a soccer player." Anne winked at Miranda.

"Or a soccer *team.*" Meg, who had twin boys, Luke and Chance, grinned impishly.

"Oh, no. Pilar and Zach are the ones working on a team," Kelly said.

Pilar's dark eyes warmed. "That's true. If everything goes according to plan, the adoption proceedings will be final and Adriana and Eduardo will be part of our family by Thanksgiving."

"Did you need anything else?" Miranda took advantage of the tiny break in conversation.

Meg and Pilar exchanged a look.

"This is going to sound strange," Meg said. "But can we get a breakfast plate to go? Rachel shouldn't have to miss out on our weekly waffles and gabfest just because she's on bed rest."

"We're all going over to her house after we eat," Pilar added. "I told Eli not to feed her…much."

"Let me know about ten minutes before you leave

and I'll put it together." Miranda was always amazed by the love and genuine concern that bonded the women together. The only person she'd ever been that close with was her sister, Lorraine. There had been several women near her age working at the bank, but Hal's possessive streak had discouraged her from pursuing any friendship with them.

"Will someone please give thanks for this meal before I faint face-first into my scrambled eggs?" Kelly moaned.

"I will." Meg chuckled as they all joined hands, completely at ease with each other and their faith.

Miranda couldn't walk away now without disrupting Meg's prayer. She glanced down self-consciously at the floor when the women bowed their heads.

"Lord, we love You. And we trust You," Meg murmured. "We trust Your protection and Your faithfulness even though we don't know what tomorrow will bring. Thank You for this food. Bless the hands that prepared and served it. Amen."

There was that word again. *Trust.*

Can I trust you, God?

The question escaped like steam from the vault of pain and doubt that had taken up residence in Miranda's heart. How long had it been since she'd talked to God? Would God even hear her anymore? Or did He only listen to women like Sandra, who'd clung to Him when things had gone wrong instead of walking away?

She looked up and found Anne's compassionate gaze resting on her.

"Don't forget about the Fourth of July celebration," Anne reminded her. "It starts at noon."

"Olivia would love to play with Daniel," Leah chimed in. Her warm smile was reflected in the faces around the table and for the first time, Miranda didn't let her experiences from the past sever the fragile connection she felt with the women gathered there.

She knew Daniel would enjoy spending the afternoon with the friends he'd made at church the week before.

"All right. We'll be there."

She said the words before she could change her mind.

Chapter Ten

Pastor Fraser recruited Andrew to join a baseball team the minute he walked through the entrance of Winchester Park. In the name of patriotism and to identify him as a "Firecracker," Andrew had been given a red-white-and-blue striped baseball cap. Which looked ridiculous. He might have complained if Ross hadn't sidled up to him, wearing a "crown" made out of green foam that looked suspiciously like the one Lady Liberty wore.

"Humbling, isn't it?" Ross muttered. "I want to hunt down the person responsible for this."

Andrew's gaze scanned the park. "Just so there aren't any reporters lurking around today."

Ross lifted an eyebrow. "I hate to be the one to break this to you, but they're going to be swarming the place later. Jared mentioned that Douglas Matthews is going to be here. His show is going national, you know, so he's big news now. Hometown boy becomes successful television personality."

"Let's make him an honorary Firecracker. I'll give him my hat."

"I respect a man who puts the needs of others first." Ross grinned.

"Andrew, Ross, we're ready to start." Scott Crosby, the associate pastor of Chestnut Grove Community, waved a baseball bat in the air to get their attention.

"Time to separate the men from the boys." Andrew tipped his hat at Ross.

"Take it easy on me, Noble. I'm an old married man now, you know." Ross blew a kiss to Kelly, who sat at a nearby picnic table with Sandra Lange. Seated next to Sandra was an older gentleman whose snow-white hair and Hawaiian-print shirt made him look like Santa Claus on summer holiday. Andrew recognized him as Tony Conlon, the owner of Conlon's Gift Emporium.

Andrew had almost reached the dugout when a small whirlwind in a green T-shirt intercepted him. Daniel. Without thinking, he scooped him up and tossed him over one shoulder.

"Hey, bud. I didn't think I'd see you here today." But he'd been hoping.

Daniel's words were muffled against Andrew's shoulder.

"What?" Andrew shouted. "I can't hear you. You have to speak up."

"Mom's. Over. There." A giggle punctuated each word.

The sound of his laughter pierced Andrew right down to the bone. How had this little guy and his mom gotten under his skin so quickly?

"Where?" Andrew spun in a circle, turning Daniel into a human wind sock before depositing him on the ground once again.

Daniel pointed to a tree not far from the ball field. Miranda sat underneath it on a colorful blanket. Alone. The sunlight filtered through the trees, coaxing out russet highlights in her hair. He could tell she was watching them but his spirits lifted, knowing Daniel must have had her blessing to come over and say hello.

"I better go get her." Andrew winked at him. "We need her on first base. I hope you brought your glove."

"We can play?" A wide grin split Daniel's face. "Both of us?"

"Are you kidding? Everybody gets to play today." Andrew yanked the hat off his head and put it on Daniel's. "You are now officially a Firecracker. I'll be right back."

Miranda rose to her feet when he jogged over, her expression uncertain. He wasn't surprised. He hadn't been back to the diner since he'd walked out on her at the church Friday evening. It hadn't been stubbornness that had kept him away—it was pure self-protection.

He might not have seen her in person but she'd been in his thoughts and his prayers all weekend. On Saturday morning, when he'd pried a charred blueberry bagel out of the toaster, he'd wondered if she had the weekend off or if she was working. On Saturday night he'd watched *Field of Dreams* with Rachel and Eli and remembered how Miranda had briefly opened up to him when she'd tried to give the baseball glove back. Even Pastor Fraser's sermon on Sunday morning about the lost sheep had brought her to mind. If there was anyone wandering from the care and concern of the shepherd and the rest of the fold, it was Miranda Jones.

"Anne Williams invited us," Miranda said instead of hello.

Anne might have invited her, but she'd accepted the invitation.

Thank you, Anne.

The knot that had formed in his stomach over the weekend loosened a little. It was as if God was reassuring him that He was reaching out to her. Just like the message in Reverend Fraser's sermon, He was seeking out the lamb that had wandered away. Miranda was alone and afraid of something. And she didn't trust easily. He hoped that her willingness to attend the church picnic meant she was ready to open her heart a little.

"Come on. The Firecrackers need you."

"I don't know..."

"There aren't too many people brave enough to risk life and limb and slide into home plate."

A reluctant smile lifted the corners of her mouth.

"You'll have fun. Trust me." He said the words without weighing their meaning but the shadow in Miranda's eyes told him she was replaying their last conversation in her mind.

If it had been anyone else, he would have grabbed her hand and pulled her along. Not with Miranda. He held out his hand and waited.

She hesitated only a second. And then she wove her fingers through his.

* * *

"Admit it, Anne, these games are part of a diabolical plot to work up everyone's appetites so there are no leftovers," Kelly said as she squeezed between Miranda and Sandra at the picnic table.

"I don't need games to work up an appetite," Tony Conlon chuckled. "All I need is a whiff of Sandra's cooking and that does it for me."

Sandra's cheeks instantly turned pink and Miranda smiled when Tony gave the rest of the women at the table a broad wink.

After the Firecrackers triumphant win, Sandra had offered her a seat in the shade and a tall glass of lemonade while Andrew took Daniel to the other side of the park for the children's games.

The flash of disbelief in Andrew's eyes when she'd given Daniel permission to go without her had weighted her down with guilt. She hadn't expected she had the power to hurt Andrew but somehow she had. She'd gotten so used to second-guessing people's motives—she'd immediately thought the worst when Andrew had tried to befriend them—that he felt sorry for them and when the novelty passed, he'd move on. She wanted to believe it was Andrew's reputation that made her wary but she knew she couldn't put the blame entirely on that. She'd lived so long in the shadow of her secrets, it felt safer to stay there than to venture into the unknown. And a man like Andrew Noble definitely fell into the category of the unknown.

She'd memorized an apology but Andrew hadn't come into the diner all weekend. She tried to convince herself the wave of relief that had washed through her when Daniel had pointed to Andrew by the baseball field was due to the fact that she had another opportunity to make things right, not because she'd missed him.

"I know for a fact teenagers don't need to do anything to work up an appetite," Anne said. "My grocery budget doubled since Dylan came to live with us."

"Are you taking notes, Miranda?" Trista Van Zandt asked ruefully, nuzzling her son Aidan's plump cheek. "I can't imagine this little guy outgrowing his strained fruits and veggies."

When Kelly had introduced the young woman who'd joined them at the table as Ross's younger sister, Miranda had immediately seen the resemblance between the two siblings. Ross and Trista shared the striking combination of midnight-black hair and dark blue eyes.

Trista had mentioned she'd moved to Chestnut Grove to be closer to Kelly and Ross, but Miranda recognized the haunted look in her eyes. Aidan lay cradled in the protective circle of her arms and her ring finger was bare.

"They grow up too fast," Miranda agreed, remembering how small Daniel's bicycle looked and his need for new clothing.

Kelly glanced at her watch and stood up. "It's getting close to one, so I better go and rustle up the dessert I brought. Teenage boys aren't the only ones with a sweet tooth, you know. I had to hide the cake from Ross this morning so he wouldn't snitch a piece. All in the name of a *taste test,* of course."

Anne dropped a kiss on the top of Christina's head,

stirring her daughter's golden curls. "Let's go tell your daddy it's time to eat, shall we?"

"Is there anything I can do to help?" Miranda asked, feeling surprisingly at ease with the women gathered around the table.

"I've got some lawn chairs in the trunk that Ross made me promise I wouldn't try to carry," Kelly said. "If you can grab those, I'll bring the cake."

"Let me go tell Andrew and Daniel. I'll be right back." Miranda stood up, smoothed the wrinkles out of her cotton shorts and tucked a strand of hair behind one ear.

"You look beautiful, sugar," Sandra whispered.

Miranda's cheeks flamed. It suddenly occurred to her that Sandra might try to take on the role of matchmaker. Between her and Andrew. Which was laughable. Even though she'd begun to sense that a core of integrity and kindness lay beneath Andrew's veneer of charm, it didn't mean he was interested in her.

As Miranda carefully made her way through the colorful maze of picnic blankets spread on the ground, a group of people jostled past her.

"Excuse us. Coming through."

"Look! There he is. And he's got the whole family with him today," one of the men in the group crowed.

"Perfect." A wraithlike woman with platinum-blond hair brushed past Miranda, churning the air with the cloying scent of her perfume. "Set up underneath those trees. Hopefully he'll give us an interview, too."

At first Miranda thought they were talking about Andrew but as they veered away from the cluster of people from Chestnut Grove Community Church, she realized their quarry was someone else. Douglas Matthews. Even though he lived in the area, Miranda had never seen him in person before. The man's charismatic good looks and humorous dialogue with his guests made his afternoon talk show a favorite with the customers at the diner.

Miranda noticed Douglas wasn't exactly dressed for a hot summer day in the park—he was dressed to impress. Navy blue slacks paired with a short-sleeved white shirt set off his tanned skin and crystal-blue eyes. She wasn't surprised he had such a following. He appealed to women with his Hollywood good looks while he came across as the buddy next door—the one who generously loaned out his tools—to the men who watched his show.

A cluster of women pressed closer to him, armed with paper and pens, hoping for an autograph. Miranda suddenly noticed a woman standing several yards away from him. Light brown hair cut in a stylish bob framed her pale face but the ankle-length skirt and loose-fitting blouse seemed dated. A little boy about four or five years old—a miniature replica of Douglas—clung to her leg.

Douglas frequently made references to his family on television but somehow Miranda had expected his wife to be as vivacious and camera-ready as he was.

"Mr. Matthews!" The platinum-blonde parted the crowd gathered around Douglas. "Can we get some pictures? And maybe an interview?"

"Veronica, how did you find me here?" The disapproving shake of his head belied the satisfied look in his eyes.

"I followed your adoring fans," Veronica said, a flirtatious smile curving her lips.

"I don't know—" Douglas was playing hard to get "—this is a family outing today. I'm not really prepared for an interview."

"So, we'll take some pictures of your family, too." Veronica motioned to the photographer checking the settings on his digital camera. She sashayed over to the boy and bent down.

"The camera loves little Logan as much as it does his daddy," she cooed.

"Lynda? Is this all right with you?" Douglas asked, his voice low and solicitous.

Lynda Matthews gave a hesitant nod. Apparently, there was some truth to the old adage *opposites attract.* Miranda couldn't imagine two more different personalities. Douglas courted attention while Lynda seemed almost afraid of it.

"Douglas, let's get one of you with your son."

Lynda had to peel Logan away from her leg. Douglas's lips flattened as the boy immediately tried to scramble back to his mother.

"The three of you together, then." Veronica's critical gaze swept over Lynda and now she looked less than pleased to have to include her in the shot.

Douglas picked up a squirming Logan and whispered something in his ear. The boy stilled in his father's arms and ducked his head.

"Star gazing?" A low voice at Miranda's shoulder made her jump.

Andrew. With Daniel happily perched on his strong shoulders as if he was meant to be there. An arrow of pure longing pierced Miranda. Maybe it was selfish to claim this day with Andrew but when she'd watched him walking toward her earlier, something had stirred in a dormant region of her heart. Something that felt suspiciously like hope.

It made her feel younger. And a little giddy.

"Are you feeling left out?" she whispered. "I'm sure Veronica would let you pose with Douglas and his family if you asked her nicely."

"You're making fun of me." Andrew's voice was full of wonder.

"Uh-huh." She peeked up at him, unable to deny it.

"Thank you." The tender look in Andrew's eyes ripped the breath from her lungs.

Miranda wasn't about to ask what he meant by those cryptic words. Out of the corner of her eye she saw Douglas curve his arm around Lynda's slim waist, Logan huddled between them, as flashbulbs went off like a miniature fireworks display.

A prickle skittered up the back of Miranda's neck. There was something unsettling about the perfect family moment the cameras vied to capture. Douglas's smile radiated rakish charm but Lynda's pale skin had a waxy sheen, making her pale blue eyes look huge. And Logan…Miranda had seen the same look of helpless terror in Daniel's face when Hal had shoved her against the wall.

Miranda pushed away the dark thoughts as another example of how she'd let the past taint the way she viewed the world. Logan was young. Just because Douglas thrived in the limelight didn't mean his family was comfortable with it.

"Me and Olivia won the three-legged race." Daniel bounced up and down on Andrew's shoulders, drawing her attention away from Lynda and Logan Matthews for the moment.

When Daniel leaned over so she could admire the gold medal hanging from a satin ribbon around his neck, Andrew wrapped one tanned forearm around Daniel's knees to keep him steady.

"And now he's hungry, aren't you, champ?"

"Daniel Thomas, where did you put all those pancakes you had for breakfast this morning?" Miranda tweaked his toes. "I thought they'd fill you up until suppertime."

"That explains why he's so heavy. I thought it was the medal." Andrew smiled at her and she knew why women found him irresistible.

Maybe she should call it a day while her heart was still in one piece....

"Are you hungry, Mom?" Daniel's eyes pleaded with her to stay longer.

"A little." Just because Andrew had coerced them into playing baseball didn't mean he wanted to spend the entire day with them. "I told Kelly I'd help her carry some chairs from her car but I can take Daniel with me. You've spent a lot of time with him already. You must be here with...someone."

She'd seen Samantha Harcourt intercept Andrew as he and Daniel had made their way across the field. Rumor had it that the gorgeous runway model had recently moved back to Chestnut Grove. The familiar way the two of them greeted each other hadn't surprised Miranda. They both came from a background of wealth and privilege and probably shared the same circle of friends.

She couldn't blame Andrew for wanting to spend time with a woman like Samantha. A woman more comfortable at one of the Noble Foundation's galas than the kitchen of the Starlight Diner....

"As a matter of fact, I am. I'm here with you."

Andrew offered her his arm as elegantly as any Southern gentleman would have. And, at that moment, it seemed the most natural thing in the world to take hold of it.

Chapter Eleven

Kelly looked relieved when Miranda and Andrew returned with the chairs. "Trista went to track down Ross for me. Can you keep an eye on Aidan until we get back?" Without waiting for an answer, she plunked her nephew into Andrew's arms and towed Miranda away.

"I watched him with Daniel." Kelly smiled when she noticed the wide-eyed look Miranda tossed over her shoulder. "For a confirmed bachelor, he's a natural with kids. Have you two been seeing each other very long?"

"I… He… We're…not seeing each other." Miranda practically choked on the words. "That was Andrew Noble," she added. Just in case Kelly hadn't recognized him. Which seemed impossible, given the fact they were living on the same planet.

"I know who it was." Kelly grinned. "But Rachel… Oh, never mind. Put a gaggle of happily married women together and we start pairing off everyone we know and care about."

"Rachel?" Miranda repeated. *Rachel Cavanaugh?* Andrew's cousin. The cousin on bed rest who'd never even *seen* her and Andrew together.

It made her uneasy to think she'd become the topic of conversation. Especially since she'd gone out of her way over the last few years to be as invisible as possible.

"There's my car." Kelly deftly changed the subject. She paused to pull a scrap of yellow paper out from under her windshield wiper. "If this is a parking ticket, Zach is going to hear about it...."

She suddenly wilted against the car door. Miranda moved to her side in a heartbeat, alarmed by the grayish cast of Kelly's skin. "Kelly? What's the matter?"

"Not again," Kelly's whispered, closing her eyes. "God, please don't tell me we're going to have to go through this again."

"Let's find a place for you to sit down," Miranda urged. "Are you having contractions?"

Kelly's hands moved protectively over her abdomen and the piece of paper fluttered from her fingers. Automatically, Miranda bent down and picked it up. The two sentences were neatly typed, which somehow made the message more chilling.

Make your husband stop nosing around in other people's business. Or I will.

"What..." Miranda swallowed hard as past events came rushing back.

The discovery of the first falsified sets of adoption records and the potential scandal they'd created for Chestnut Grove's own mayor, Gerald Morrow, had triggered his wife's emotional breakdown. Lindsey Morrow was still serving time for murdering Barnaby Harcourt and making several attempts on Kelly's life.

Helplessly, Miranda put a comforting arm around Kelly's shoulders. Was someone playing a sick joke on Kelly…or was history about to repeat itself?

"Will you find Ross?" Kelly asked, struggling to maintain her composure. "I'll be fine. I'll wait in the car."

Miranda hesitated, not wanting to leave her alone in the parking lot, but when Kelly squeezed her hand, the ice-cold press of her fingers convinced Miranda to do what she'd asked.

"All right." Miranda sprinted back toward the picnic area where most of the congregation had gathered for the cookout. She couldn't believe someone would be cruel enough to threaten Kelly Van Zandt, especially knowing her baby was due in a few short months.

Slowing her pace to scan the crowd of faces, she caught a glimpse of Trista Van Zandt. Sheltered by a canopy of trees some distance from the rest of the picnickers, Ross's sister was deep in conversation with someone. Miranda hoped it was Ross, but when she got closer she recognized Douglas Matthew's wife, Lynda.

Now what?

"Miranda? Is everything all right?" Andrew was suddenly beside her.

"No." Her voice wobbled. "I need your help."

Kelly was pale but composed by the time Miranda and Andrew returned to the parking lot with Ross and Sandra.

Ross wasn't. He read the note, his eyes dark with fury.

"Ross, we have to tell Zach about this," Kelly murmured.

"Pilar's husband." Miranda caught Andrew's questioning look. "He's a detective with the police department."

Kelly heard her and managed a smile. "And a good one."

"I'll call him, but right now I'm going to take you home." The tightness in Ross's jaw softened slightly when he returned his wife's smile.

Miranda blinked back the sudden rush of tears that burned the back of her eyes. Tears that didn't make sense. She barely knew Kelly and Ross other than as customers at the diner.

"I'm going with you." Sandra wrapped her arm around Kelly's shoulders and drew her close.

Ross turned to Miranda. "Thank you," he said simply. "I'm glad you were with her."

Andrew felt the shift in Miranda's mood as Ross drove away with Kelly and Sandra, but this time he was determined not to let her retreat behind the walls she'd built. He wasn't sure what shook him up the most. That Miranda didn't seem to know how to accept a simple expression of gratitude or the empathy in her eyes when she'd looked at Kelly. An empathy that told him she understood what it was like to be threatened by someone.

"Someone sent the note because of the adoption records Jonah Fraser found, right?" They were halfway back to the picnic area when she finally spoke.

"I don't know." He had a strong hunch but something in her expression warned him to tread carefully. "Harcourt accepted a lot of money so certain families wouldn't have any scandals attached to their names. New records are a new threat to those families—especially if they turn out to be the originals."

"Like Ben's."

Andrew nodded as they fell in step together.

"I think Daniel and I should go home." Miranda wouldn't look at him now.

God, what is it going to take to get through to this woman?

"And miss the fireworks? Daniel's been talking about them all day." He kept his tone light. "But if you really want to, I suppose we could leave early."

"We?" She frowned at him.

"I told you I was with you today. If you're here, I'm here. If you go home, I'll take you home."

She caught her lower lip between her teeth. "We'll stay for the fireworks."

Thank you, Lord.

Andrew knew whom to give the credit to. The two steps forward, three steps back routine with Miranda drove him a little crazy. No one could accuse him of a lack of self-confidence but Miranda tipped him off balance with every wary glance she cast in his direction.

They passed a crowd of people gathered around Douglas Matthews again. Now the talk-show host stood on a makeshift stage with a large plastic bib tied around his neck, responding to the good-natured heckling from the audience. An attractive woman postured next to him for the cameras, holding a pie. The local businesses had organized a pie-eating contest and

Douglas. had somehow charmed his way into the competition.

One of the photographers circling the contestants suddenly noticed them. Andrew had quickly learned that hiding from the press or refusing to be photographed only made him more of a challenge. He didn't want their attention but he accepted it. They had an unspoken agreement of sorts. He smiled at the cameras in public and they didn't encroach too much in his private life. And that was the life he needed to protect.

The photographer grinned, snapped their picture and raised his camera in a cheerful salute.

Andrew shot a look at Miranda but her attention was focused on Daniel, who chased after Olivia and some other children in a lively game of tag. He decided not to mention they'd just been preserved in someone's memory card. Miranda was skittish enough about being seen with him.

Miranda tried to remain invisible.

In a group as large as the one sprawled on the red-white-and-blue quilts Naomi Fraser and her daughter, Dinah, had spread out in the shade of a massive oak, it should have been easy to go unnoticed.

Wrong.

Even though Miranda worked her way to a corner of the blanket, hoping to avoid the overlapping threads of conversation, people included her in the conversation with a comment here, a question there.

Daniel, her usual buffer in social situations, abandoned her after the teens in Caleb's youth group had descended upon the younger children and divided them into teams for a water-balloon fight.

Her first response was to say no. Water made grass wet and slippery, which meant Daniel might fall down and get hurt.

"He'll be fine," Andrew whispered in her ear. "If he falls down, he'll get back up, Miranda."

She wasn't sure what was more unsettling. That he read her thoughts or that her pulse went crazy when his lips grazed her ear.

"...so I heard the nurse ask, 'Are you all right?' and I told her I was doing fine. Then I realized she was looking at Ben!" Leah's lilting voice rose above the hum of conversation.

Several masculine groans followed.

"Buckle up, guys. It's time for the afternoon segment of *Labor and Delivery*." Ben sighed.

Leah grinned and poked him in the ribs.

"Zach turned a little green during the last birthing film we watched in Lamaze class," Pilar teased. "Even though he gave a young couple a police escort to the hospital one day and had ended up delivering their baby by the side of the road instead."

"That baby wasn't mine," Zach muttered. "Do we have to talk about this?"

A rousing chorus of *yes* burst from the women huddled together on the quilt.

"We have to ask the experts so we're not nervous," Pilar said. "Anne, Meg and Leah have been through this already."

"So has Miranda," Anne reminded them.

All eyes turned to Miranda, who froze like a deer trapped in the headlights of a car.

"How long were you in labor with Daniel?" Pilar asked.

Color rushed into Miranda's face and she choked out a word no one understood.

Empathetic sighs pierced the sudden quiet.

"A difficult labor?" Naomi Fraser reached out and patted Miranda's knee. "I can relate." She gave her daughter, Dinah, a pointed look. "This one was so anxious to see the world she decided to make her appearance a month early."

"Naomi had thought she had indigestion." Pastor Fraser chuckled and raised his wife's hand to his lips. He deposited a tender kiss on her wedding ring. "Dinah was almost a roadside baby, too."

"Dad!" Dinah rolled her eyes.

The conversation shifted to another topic and Miranda drew a ragged breath, relieved she was no longer the center of attention. Heart pounding, she scooted farther into the shadow of the tree, wishing she hadn't committed to watching the fireworks. That meant two more hours in the company of friendly people who wanted her to feel included.

Fortunately, she'd managed to evade answering Anne's innocent question without lying....

This is why you don't do friendship, Miranda Jones.

"I think someone's asleep," Andrew murmured as the last shower of golden sparks dissolved in the air above their heads.

Miranda brushed the hair off Daniel's forehead and

saw that his eyes were closed. "I'm not surprised," she whispered. "It's way past his bedtime."

"You walked here, right?"

"Yes." She gave Daniel's shoulder a gentle shake but Andrew put his hand over hers.

"Don't wake him up. I'll take you home."

"We only live a few blocks away."

Andrew wasn't going to argue with her. He rose to his feet, his lean, muscular frame a dark silhouette as he draped Daniel over his shoulder. "Where am I going?"

Miranda knew she couldn't wrestle Daniel away from him. So she gave in. "Two streets behind the diner."

"Forget my car, then. It'll be quicker to carry him there than wait for everyone to leave the parking lot."

Miranda hurried to keep up so she wouldn't lose them in the mass exodus from the park. Echoes of laughter and the low hum of voices faded the farther they walked from Main Street.

Most of the houses on Magnolia Avenue were occupied by elderly people who hadn't been able to afford to move or invest in renovations. They lined the street in a mismatched row, like faded quilts on a clothesline.

"Up or down?" There was a strange inflection in Andrew's voice when they walked up the narrow cobbled sidewalk to the front door. A light glowed in the window on the second story but darkness cloaked the rest of the house.

Miranda's stomach knotted. "Up. But I'll take him...."

Andrew's eyebrow rose.

"You can look really *imperious* when you put your

mind to it," she grumbled. "Did they teach you how to do that at private school?"

Andrew's teeth flashed. Daniel stirred in his sleep and Andrew shifted him more comfortably into the crook of his arm as he followed her up the narrow flight of stairs.

Miranda replayed her morning routine. Had she left the breakfast dishes in the sink? A pair of shoes under the coffee table?

"Daniel's bedroom is on the right."

Andrew brushed past her, stirring the tangy scent of his cologne, mingled with sunshine and warm grass. Reminders of the day they'd spent together. A day she hadn't wanted to end.

Daniel's tiny bedroom seemed to shrink even more with Andrew in it. Miranda moved Lily out of the way and turned back the covers, watching as Andrew laid Daniel down and carefully pulled off his battered tennis shoes. As if tucking a child into bed was something he'd done a thousand times. The image was so different from that of the carefree, irresponsible player that for a moment, Miranda could almost picture him as a husband and father. Almost.

Daniel's eyes flickered open and focused sleepily on Andrew's face.

"Go back to sleep, champ," Andrew said softly. "You're home now. Safe and sound."

Obediently, Daniel rolled over, wrapped one arm around Lily and closed his eyes. In less than ten seconds, he was asleep again.

Miranda backed quietly out of the room, leaving the

door open a few inches so she could hear Daniel if he needed her during the night.

The apartment was quiet. So quiet that Miranda wondered if Andrew could hear the wild thumping of her heart. She assumed he would leave after seeing them back safely, but instead, he took a leisurely lap around the living room.

"Have you and Daniel lived here very long?" He paused in front of a curio cabinet where a flock of glass birds nested. She didn't share Mrs. Enderby's love of antique salt-and-pepper mills, but it didn't feel right to pack away things that belonged to her landlady. And it wasn't as if she had anything to replace them.

"A few years."

He wasn't fast enough to hide his surprise at her answer. And Miranda knew why. As if a curtain had been pulled aside, she saw the apartment through someone else's eyes. *His* eyes.

When Miranda had answered the ad in the newspaper, she'd considered it a plus that it was furnished. Never mind it was furnished with an eclectic blend of Mrs. Enderby's castoffs. When she and Daniel had left Atlanta, only the things that fit in the trunk of her car had gone with them.

As time went on, she'd learned to live with Mrs. Enderby's velveteen sofa and the mismatched china in the cabinets. She didn't have the money to spend on things they might have to leave behind. The only personal items on display were Daniel's school picture in a homemade frame and the bouquet of fresh daisies on the scarred kitchen table. The fresh flowers she purchased every week not only lifted her spirits but gave the dreary room a face-lift. They were a temporary treasure—one she could enjoy but walk away from if necessary.

"Where did you and Daniel live before you moved to Chestnut Grove?" Andrew moved on to study the garish oil painting of a seascape that took up most of the wall.

She'd taken it down once and saw it had been strategically placed there to cover a large tear in the wallpaper. So back it had gone.

Miranda's shoulders tightened. All afternoon and during the fireworks, Daniel had been a lively buffer between them. But not anymore. Now she was aware of how late it was. And there was no barrier protecting her from Andrew's innocent questions. When Sandra had hired her at the diner, Miranda had compiled a list of vague responses to satisfy any questions a person might ask. Ordinary questions. But there was nothing ordinary about Andrew Noble or his questions. And his intent gaze had her scrambling to remember the answers.

"South of here." Honest if a bit misleading. Georgia *was* south of Virginia.

"Do you still have family? South of here?" His knowing look gently mocked her answer.

What did he want from her?

"No." She still felt the pain of Lorraine's absence like a wound that wouldn't heal.

Her parents had divorced shortly after she'd graduated from high school. Her father's company had transferred him to Japan, where he'd started a new life but remembered to send her a birthday card every year. Her mother had remarried a career military officer who wanted a wife but wasn't interested in two daughters. He'd conveniently pretended she and Lorraine didn't exist. Even before Lorraine's death, their mother had gradually been withdrawing from their lives.

Daniel was the only family she had.

Andrew picked up the current issue of a finance magazine and scanned the cover. "Light reading?"

"It's a coaster." The scowl she sent in his direction backfired. His soft laughter filled the empty corners of the room. And her heart.

"I'm...tired." It was the truth. She was tired. And confused. And afraid he was getting too close.

Her breath caught in her throat when he took a step toward her, but all he did was tuck a strand of hair behind her ear. The gentle brush of his fingertips against her cheek was more comforting than intimate.

"Good night, Miranda." He smiled. "Breakfast at eight."

The snick of the door closing behind him jolted Miranda out of the semicoma the touch of his fingers had put her in. She slumped into the old tweed recliner and buried her face in her hands. When she looked up again, the soft glow under the yellowed lamp shade somehow made the room look even more dreary and neglected.

Home. Safe and sound. That was what Andrew had told Daniel. But the irony of his words wasn't lost on her. She hadn't made the apartment a home. For four years she'd lived in a state of limbo just in case she'd had to take Daniel and leave again.

Treasured photos of Lorraine and Tom were still in a box under the bed. The furnishings couldn't even be considered a twist on the popular "shabby chic" decor. They were just shabby.

She'd ignored the urge to ask Mrs. Enderby for permission to paint over the water-stained vanilla walls in the kitchen or give the rickety dining-room chairs a decent burial.

She'd set all her hopes on an elusive "someday." Someday she and Daniel would have a house with a big backyard and a basketball hoop. Someday she wouldn't have to buy flowers; she'd grow her own. Someday she would pick out furniture in the shades of rose and yellow and green she loved.

Her gaze settled on the narrow closet set in the wall between the living room and the kitchen. Somehow, the two suitcases behind the door had come to define their lives.

And she was tired of it.

She walked over to the large window overlooking the street and gathered up a fistful of dusty brocade. The heavy pinch-pleated drapes, in a shade of orange that reminded her of rusty water, would have looked more at home in the great room of a medieval castle.

She pulled a chair up to the window and reached up on her tiptoes, methodically yanking out the silver pins holding the curtains in place. Dust tickled her nose but she didn't quit. Not until the last of the panels slid to the floor at her feet.

Her fingers traced the intricate, diamond-shaped panels of leaded glass that framed the wide pane. And the window ledge was deep enough to sit on. Almost. She teetered on the edge and braced one foot against the chair to keep herself steady as she rested her cheek against the glass.

The pale glow of a streetlamp captured the shaggy silhouettes of the trees and softened the lines of the houses. And, for the first time, she could see the stars.

Chapter Twelve

Sandra was awake most of the night but lost sleep didn't bother her as much as it used to. Instead of tossing and turning and worrying that she'd look like a zombie the next day, her perspective had changed. Now she looked at it as an opportunity to pray.

She unlocked the back door of the diner and the musical jingle of the keys drew her attention to the pink bracelet around her wrist.

"You're right, Lord. We've been through a lot," she said out loud. "But I have to tell you I'd rather go through trials and tribulation than watch the people I love go through them. Why is that? When I know that in the darkest places, Your love shines the brightest?"

After leaving the park the day before, she'd spent the rest of the afternoon and evening with Kelly and Ross.

After the initial shock of finding the note had worn off, Ross had switched into what Kelly often teasingly referred to as "Colombo" mode. He'd called Jared Kierney to find out if he knew who'd written the letters to the editor that had appeared in the *Gazette* the week before. One of the letters had blamed the Harcourt family for Barnaby's illegal activities and the other had insinuated Kelly had deliberately tried to suppress information about the latest documents that had been discovered.

Even though the *Gazette* was running on a skeleton crew because of the holiday, Jared had called back within the hour. Both letters had come in on the same day via snail mail and both had Richmond postmarks stamped on the envelopes. That narrowed it down to roughly two-hundred-thousand people.

Jared had promised to figure out a way to do some damage control even if it meant interviewing Kelly again to clear up some of the misconceptions the letters had created.

His promise had done little for Kelly's peace of mind. Sandra had prayed with both her and Ross before she'd left but she knew Kelly was in a battle against fear. Not for herself, but for Ross. And their unborn child.

"Sandra? Is everything all right?"

With a start, Sandra heard Miranda's voice behind her. She realized the key was still in the door and she hadn't moved.

"Don't mind me." Sandra chuckled. "I was just having a little chat with God. You're here early." She pushed the door open and the smell of cinnamon and yeast rolled over them.

"So are you."

Sandra replaced her lightweight sweater with her signature pink apron and smoothed out the *S* sewn on the shoulder—a morning ritual Miranda doubted Sandra was even aware of. She didn't miss the pronounced lines fanning out from the corners of Sandra's eyes. And she knew what had put them there.

She'd always been careful not to get involved in the lives of the people she worked with. Darcy, with her flare for drama, tried to pull her into the complex web of her life on occasion, but for the most part Miranda had kept herself apart. If she encouraged people to confide in her, she might be tempted to confide in them. The seeds of friendship. And friends would be harder to leave behind than material possessions.

But even though Miranda had rebuffed her many times, Sandra had never stopped reaching out to her. And she'd thought a lot about Kelly and Ross while she'd washed every inch of the picture window. At midnight.

"How is Kelly?" she asked tentatively.

Sandra poured a cup of coffee and gave it to Miranda. "That's what I was talking to the Lord about. She went through a terrible time, you know. We all did." Her eyes clouded with memories. "Lindsey Morrow could have killed Kelly. And now someone else… I just don't want her to go through this again. The adoption agency has been flourishing the past few years because of her and Eric's dedication, and she and Ross are so excited about the baby…."

Miranda took her employer's hand without thinking. "Maybe they should go away for a while."

Sandra's eyes widened. "Go away?"

"Take a trip somewhere. Or maybe even move."

"Chestnut Grove is Kelly's home," Sandra said gently. "Her friends are here. Her church family is here. Her parents are buried here. Her *life* is here."

"But it's not safe." Couldn't Sandra see that? This was her daughter they were talking about.

"Sugar, the safest place to be is in God's hands. And that's where Kelly and Ross and my future grandbaby are. I've always believed that if a person runs away, they never leave their troubles behind—they only bring them along."

God's hands.

Daniel's Bible verse played through Miranda's mind like the words to a song. *See, I have engraved you on the palms of my hands.*

Who was that true for? People who did everything right? People who'd believed God and never strayed off His path?

"But how do you know you can trust God? You battled cancer. Kelly almost died a few years ago because of Lindsey Morrow. You weren't able to have more children—" Miranda couldn't prevent the words that tumbled out but she didn't understand how Sandra could still trust.

"Sometimes when we're struggling, the enemy wants us to believe that God takes things away from us. That isn't true. God wants to *give* us things. Beauty for ashes. Joy for mourning. Strength for fear." Sandra smiled. "What if Daniel ran away from you when he got hurt instead of coming to you for help? It would break your heart. It isn't so different with God, Miranda. I can trust Him because I know He loves me." She opened up the palms of her hands. "I'm right here. Remember?"

* * *

"Mr. Noble." Zoe caught up with Andrew at the elevator. There's someone here to see you."

"I don't have time now, Zoe. Did you ask them to reschedule? I've got an appointment with Josiah Chrone in fifteen minutes." He punched the button on the elevator, impatient to get the meeting over with. Zoe had called him at home that morning to tell him Mr. Chrone had insisted they meet for breakfast at his home. Which meant Andrew hadn't been able to stop at the diner to see Miranda.

But he couldn't pass up the "invitation." He hadn't made a lot of progress with the elusive Mr. Chrone. The elderly widower had a generous heart for the needy and a soft spot for Rachel. Somehow, both of those things combined to create an unexpected stubbornness when it came to dealing with Andrew.

They'd talked on the phone several times and even met for lunch once but they still hadn't found a point of connection. The point of connection that would gain Josiah's trust and make him feel comfortable enough to give the Noble Foundation a sizable donation, earmarked for college scholarships to underprivileged high-school students.

Andrew knew, if he needed to, he could enlist Rachel's help. Connecting with people was one of her gifts. And, no doubt, she could accomplish it from her cell phone. On bed rest. Exactly the reason why Andrew wasn't going to ask her. He'd overheard the employees discussing the situation around the water cooler. For all he knew, they were keeping score. He hated to admit it, but his pride was at stake.

Zoe looked guilty. And frazzled. "I did mention you were leaving."

"And?" The door swished open and Andrew took a step forward.

Zoe leaped in front of him, blocking his path.

Andrew blinked.

"He said he would wait."

The doors closed again. Now he was late. Mr. Chrone didn't appreciate *late.*

He sighed. Nothing that torpedoed his day was that important. Not if it wasn't accompanied by a certain ring tone on his cell phone. "Who is it, Zoe?"

"I'm not sure—"

"Zoe."

"It's a little boy. He said his name is Daniel."

"Call Mr. Chrone and tell him something came up." Andrew pivoted sharply away from the elevator and strode back to his office.

It *was* Daniel. He sat in one of the high-back leather chairs in the reception area, feet dangling six inches above the floor. Both arms were wrapped around his backpack.

And he was alone.

"Hey, champ." Andrew knelt down in front of him. "Where's your mom this morning?"

Daniel ducked his head and his legs began to swing rhythmically back and forth. "Working."

Questions lined up in his mind but Andrew noticed Zoe standing in the doorway behind him, clearly fascinated at the scene unfolding in front of her.

"Zoe, are there still some pastries left in the break room?"

"Uh-huh." Her head bobbed.

"Could you bring them to my office? And a glass of milk."

"Milk?" Zoe's nose wrinkled as if she'd never heard the word.

He lifted an eyebrow.

"Yes, Mr. Noble. Milk." Zoe backed out the door and disappeared.

When the sharp clip of her stilettos faded, he turned back to Daniel. "Let's go into my office."

Daniel jumped down and Andrew noticed the swimming goggles looped around his arm.

"How did you get here, Daniel? Did Hallie bring you?" He knew Miranda was working and Sonshine Camp had officially ended. The next logical assumption was that Daniel should be with his babysitter.

Daniel shook his head. "I…walked. From the park."

Andrew quickly calculated the distance between Winchester Park and the Noble Foundation and his blood chilled. "By yourself?"

The look Daniel slid in his direction was weighted with fear but he nodded. "Mom showed me where you worked when we took a walk. And I saw your car in the parking lot."

"Does your mother know you're here?"

Tears filled Daniel's eyes and he shook his head mutely.

Andrew blew out a quiet breath. The shadows in Daniel's eyes warned him to tread carefully. "Aren't you supposed to be with Hallie this morning?"

Daniel's eyes darkened to the color of espresso behind the thick lenses of his glasses, searching for the answer to a silent question. *Could he trust him?* It was the same expression Andrew had seen on Miranda's face the night before. And it made him wonder all over again what they'd gone through.

"We met some of her friends at the park," Daniel said in a low voice. "She said I'd have fun. They had some cool stuff but if I wanted to try it, I couldn't tattle."

A code straight from the troublemaker's handbook. And ruthlessly effective on someone Daniel's age who wanted to fit in with the "big" kids. Andrew tamped down his rising anger.

"Tattling is telling on someone to get them into trouble. If a person might get hurt, telling someone is the best thing you can do. It shows you're a true friend." His mother would be thrilled to know he'd remembered one of her lectures. And it seemed to work. The shadows lifted slightly as Daniel digested the words. "What kind of cool stuff did they have?"

"Fireworks," he whispered.

Relief pulsed through Andrew. Not because fireworks weren't dangerous but because he'd automatically assumed it was something worse. Considering the Fourth of July celebration the day before, it shouldn't have surprised him that Hallie's friends had a surplus of fireworks. But it didn't explain why Daniel had left the park without Hallie. And why he'd come to him instead of going to Miranda at the diner.

"You shouldn't have left the park," Andrew said, as gently as he could. "Hallie is probably worried about you—"

"One of the kids was being mean to a dog." The

words came out in a rush. "And he got mad when I let it go. He said he was going to find it again and put it in a box and drop the firecrackers inside. I told him we wouldn't let him."

We.

The absolute certainty that Andrew was going to help him right a wrong humbled him. Daniel didn't know Andrew's reputation. He didn't know that Andrew Noble supposedly looked after only one person—himself. What was it that Miranda had told him after the closing program for Sonshine Camp? That Daniel viewed him as some kind of hero?

The faith the kid had in him was humbling. Time to don his invisible cape.

He held out his hand and Daniel grabbed it. "We better get back there, then."

On their way out, they almost bowled down Zoe.

"Hold my calls, please, Zoe." He snagged a pastry off the tray as they went past her and handed it to Daniel.

"Mr. Chrone said if you aren't on his veranda by noon with an apology and a good excuse, he's going to call Rachel at home and tell her…" Zoe craned her neck to read the piece of paper clutched in her hand "…you'll have to sell all your fancy cars to make up for the scholarship money the Foundation is going to lose."

Andrew laughed. "Call Mr. Chrone and tell him there'll be two of us…for lunch."

Miranda had given up on Andrew when he'd missed the breakfast rush. She didn't expect to see him sneak into the kitchen through the back door. With Daniel. And a tiny animal with laughing shoe-button eyes and stringy brown fur that looked as if it hadn't had a bath in months.

"Daniel, what's going on? Where is Hallie? *Yuck!*" Miranda yelped as the dog's tongue unrolled and took a friendly swipe at her cheek.

"Is that a dog?" Darcy, who'd just swept into the kitchen, stopped dead in her tracks and stared. Not at Andrew but at the furry thing in his arms.

"It's six health-code violations." Isaac's scowl was as dark as a December morning. "Get it out of my kitchen."

"Can you take five, Miranda?" One of Andrew's hands trapped the wriggling dog in the crook of his arm, the other rested on Daniel's shoulder.

"Sure she can." Sandra breezed in and cheerfully answered the question, not at all taken aback by the strange gathering in the kitchen. "Things won't pick up for another hour or so. Take your time."

Isaac rolled his eyes and flipped a pancake onto a plate. "Daniel? Do you want this one?"

"I can't. Me and Andrew have a lunch meeting. It's Take-a-Friend-to-Work Day, isn't it, Andrew?"

Miranda sagged against the counter. Smelling salts would have come in handy if they were still in fashion.

Without ceremony, Andrew took hold of her elbow and pulled her into the alley. When the screen door snapped shut behind them, Miranda put her hands on her hips.

"Explain. Why. You. Have. My. Son."

He did. By the time he was finished, Miranda wasn't sure whether to laugh or cry. So she did a little of both.

"But Hallie didn't tell me Daniel was gone."

"She thought he was hiding. She and her friends were still looking for him when I got there."

"But something could have happened. He's only seven years old!"

"We discussed that before she quit." The edge in Andrew's voice made her blink.

"She quit?"

He plowed his lean fingers through his hair, leaving it in casual disarray. "Actually, I think I fired her."

"You fired my son's babysitter."

He shot her an apologetic look. "She tried to make excuses when there weren't any. Hinted that Daniel overreacted. Said the dog was an ugly stray. Which is probably true, but that's beside the point."

"Why did he go to the Noble Foundation?" It was a poor substitute for the question she wanted to ask. *Why did he go to you?*

"He wanted me to rescue the dog."

Miranda wanted to argue that she was capable of rescuing a dog, too, but it would have sounded petty. She went for coolly polite instead. "I appreciate you taking the time from work. I'll call Hallie. Daniel can stay with me until my shift ends."

If she'd paid attention to her doubts about Hallie in the first place, Daniel wouldn't have been in a potentially dangerous situation. Even now, the thought of him walking alone to the Noble Foundation gave her a queasy feeling. There was no doubt she'd have to find someone else to care for Daniel in the mornings but she didn't know where to begin. She didn't have a network of friends to give her recommendations. She'd found

Hallie by putting an advertisement in the newspaper and that had taken several weeks.

"He's more than welcome to stay with me for a few more hours. It's Take-a-Friend-to-Work Day, you know." Andrew looked so innocent, she almost believed him.

"You made that up."

"You're giving me way too much credit." Andrew winced as his tie became too much of a temptation for the dog, who gave it a sharp tug. "I have a lunch meeting with a potential client who happens to know as many baseball statistics as your son. They'll have a lot to talk about. Mr. Chrone doesn't like me so I'm hoping Daniel will win him over."

"You've done enough for us," she argued, thoroughly charmed by the sight of Andrew's silk tie being shredded by a dog no larger than a loaf of bread. "I can't let you—"

"Miranda, it's time you let someone."

The quiet statement battered her already weakening defenses. She didn't know how he'd gained such a foothold in their life. It wasn't only Daniel's attachment to Andrew that worried her. For the first time she recognized the truth. Her heart was at risk, too.

"I'll have him back to you by three. I promise."

Two words she'd heard before. Two words she'd stopped believing. At least, she thought she had. Until now.

Reminding herself that keeping promises didn't mean a thing in Andrew Noble's world didn't help, either. Her traitorous heart no longer lined up with her head. Every time she tried to put Andrew into the same category with Hal, her memory stubbornly refused to cooperate. Instead, it replayed a series of images. Images of Andrew carrying Daniel up the stairs after the fireworks. The tender look in his eyes when he'd brushed the hair away from her face. His calm acceptance of a morning disrupted by a runaway boy and a stray dog.

She swallowed hard against the lump in her throat.

"Three o'clock."

At two minutes to three, Daniel bounded into the kitchen. Alone.

Miranda caught a glimpse of Andrew's Ferrari pulling away from the curb.

"Andrew couldn't stay, Mom," Daniel said, oblivious to the war going on inside his mother as disappointment battled against relief. "He said to give you this, though."

He handed her a single white rose.

Chapter Thirteen

"Are you sure Mrs. Enderby isn't going to get mad?" Daniel eyed the paintbrush in Miranda's hand as if he wasn't quite ready to believe they had permission for the project.

"I'm sure," Miranda answered patiently. Even though it had to be the tenth time she'd heard the question.

But she could understand Daniel's caution. Miranda had been ready to plead her case to get their landlady's permission to make changes to the apartment, so Mrs. Enderby's response had surprised her, too. The elderly woman's eyes had narrowed as she'd given Miranda a measured look and finally she'd muttered, "It's about time." She'd shocked Miranda even further by offering to reimburse her for the cost of the paint because Miranda had volunteered to do all the work.

Sandra would have smiled and declared it was God's provision. Just like Daniel's new babysitter. Leah Cavanaugh.

If Mrs. Enderby's easy acceptance of the home improvements hadn't stunned her enough, Leah had called her less than an hour later. She'd taken Olivia to the diner for ice cream, where Sandra had filled her in on Miranda's babysitter dilemma. Leah had called Ben and he'd agreed she should get in touch with Miranda as soon as possible. Since Olivia and Daniel got along so well, Leah claimed she'd be happy to watch over him while Miranda worked at the diner. And she wouldn't take no for an answer, making it sound as if Miranda would be doing *her* a favor. Joseph kept her busy and close to home, so Olivia would be thrilled to have someone to play with every day.

Daniel's excited whoop when he'd overheard parts of the conversation had convinced her that Leah and Olivia weren't the only ones who thought it was a good idea. Overwhelmed at Leah's generosity, Miranda had agreed. Starting Monday, Daniel would be going to the Cavanaughs'.

Those two bright spots managed to push back the shadow of Andrew's absence over the past two days. Her quiet little boy had turned into a chatterbox and Andrew had become his favorite topic.

Andrew had talked Mr. Chrone into adopting the stray dog.

Andrew's rearview mirror had a smiley face sticker on it.

Andrew had taken half an hour to pick out *one* flower.

Miranda's heart had stumbled over the last one. When Daniel had given her the rose, she'd assumed it was simply a casual token Andrew bestowed on all the women he knew. Or an apology for dropping Daniel off and leaving without a word.

It wasn't possible he'd chosen it especially for her because he'd noticed she loved fresh flowers. Was it?

"Let's play tic-tac-toe." Miranda needed something to take her wayward thoughts off Andrew. She dipped her brush in the paint can and laughed at the expression on her son's face.

"On the wall?" Daniel gulped and glanced over his shoulder, as if afraid Mrs. Enderby would appear in the doorway, wielding her "scolding broom."

"We're going to paint over it anyway. Come on, young man. Lighten up a little." While her mood had lifted at the thought of the work ahead of them, Daniel had gotten quieter as the morning progressed.

Daniel gifted her with a small smile and carefully painted an *X* on the grid she swiped on the wall.

Although she'd been tempted to attack the anemic beige kitchen with a gallon of paint called Primrose, she decided to paint Daniel's bedroom first. He'd lived with lavender walls long enough. It was her weekend off from the diner, which gave her a perfect opportunity to devote a large chunk of time to the project.

At the hardware store earlier that morning, Daniel had picked out a shade in an eye-popping lily-pad green. A perfect backdrop for the new comforter set they'd found at a discount store in Richmond.

"Your turn." Miranda nudged him after painting an *O* in the upper corner. They'd played tic-tac-toe enough for her to know that Daniel, a keen strategist, was usually two moves ahead of her.

Daniel dropped the brush back into the paint can. "I don't feel like playing."

"Okay." Miranda sat back on her heels, concerned. Daniel was thoughtful but rarely moody. "Let's start painting, then. If we finish by five o'clock, we'll order pizza from Gabriella's. How does that sound?"

Daniel shrugged.

Not a good sign. Thanks to Andrew and their impromptu picnic in the park that day, Daniel adored pizza from the quaint Italian restaurant.

She tried again. "Aren't you anxious to finish your new room, Danny? I thought—"

"When are we leaving?"

Miranda was confused—not only by the question but by the flash of sorrow in Daniel's eyes. "Leaving where?"

"Here." Daniel slumped on the bed and picked up Lily, snuggling the stuffed animal against his chest. "That's why we're fixing things up, isn't it?"

The air whooshed out of her lungs.

Oh, Daniel.

"Is that what you thought?" She gathered Daniel into her lap and wrapped her arms around him. "We're fixing things up for us. And for Lily. She hates the color lavender, you know. She's going to be much happier with green."

Daniel didn't smile. "But you moved the suitcases. I saw you."

Miranda's breath snagged in her throat. She hadn't

realized Daniel knew about the suitcases stashed in the closet.

What other insecurities had Daniel been harboring the last few years? He'd been three years old when they'd left Atlanta. As far as she knew, he had no memories of the place. Or the man he'd toddled after, trying to replace the father he'd lost.

"The suitcases don't mean we're leaving, Daniel." She hoped she wasn't making a promise she couldn't keep. "Chestnut Grove is…home."

Daniel sagged against her, as if hearing the words lifted a tremendous weight from his shoulders.

The strange thing was Miranda felt it, too. As if saying the words set something free inside of her.

Chestnut Grove had simply been a dot on the map the night they'd left Georgia. She'd tried to convince herself the name of the town had come to her because of Daniel's ties to Tiny Blessings, but maybe it had been the answer to the desperate cry of her heart. That she'd find a safe place for her and Daniel.

If she was brave enough to believe what Sandra said—that God hadn't forgotten her—maybe it meant He'd led them to Chestnut Grove. To the Starlight Diner. And Sandra and Isaac.

Sandra's words cycled back in her mind.

The safest place to be is in God's hands. People who run away never leave their problems behind… They only bring them along.

She'd never embraced the town as home. Had stubbornly resisted viewing it as anything more than a temporary resting place. The packed suitcases in the closet held more than their clothes. They held the memory of Hal's threats to find her if she tried to leave him and the fear of trusting the wrong people. And in many ways, herself.

"Can we unpack them?" The hopeful look in Daniel's eyes made her wince.

She didn't think she was ready for that. Maybe the fragile bonds holding her to Chestnut Grove weren't strong enough to stand against her insecurities and fear.

The safest place to be is in God's hands.

She shook the thought away, still afraid to reach out and claim it as her own. "We're all ready to paint, Daniel. We can unpack the suitcases later."

"Please, Mom. It'll only take a few minutes."

"I suppose—" Daniel's whoop drowned out the rest of the words and he scampered from the bedroom. By the time she rounded the corner seconds later, he'd already dragged the suitcases into the living room.

"Here is yours. And this one is mine." Unerringly, he pushed the plain blue suitcase toward her.

Miranda determined never to underestimate her son again. To know which one belonged to him, he must have looked inside it. How long had he known about them? Wondered about them? *Worried about them?*

Daniel flopped down onto his knees and unzipped the red case.

"Mom?" His forehead furrowed as he held up a tiny shirt, the folds sharpened with age. "I don't think this will fit me anymore."

Her mouth fell open.

Daniel pulled out a miniature pair of blue jeans and tossed them in the air. "These won't fit me, either!"

Something burst inside Miranda, releasing an avalanche of debris from the past.

Daniel had been a preschooler when they'd come to Chestnut Grove and she'd never replaced the clothing as Daniel had grown. She couldn't believe it. The suitcases had become frozen in time. Expecting the worst. Waiting.

Just like you.

Something loosened inside her. Making room for a helpless giggle.

She followed Daniel's example. Into the air went an outdated shirt—one she hadn't been too fond of when she'd bought it. She juggled two pairs of socks and then tossed them over her head before reaching for the next item.

Laughing, Miranda didn't hear the soft tap on the door. But Daniel did. He rushed to answer it and Miranda heard the familiar voice and Daniel's enthusiastic greeting.

"Hi, Andrew!"

A scarf drifted down and landed on Miranda's knee as her eyes met Andrew's.

"Are you going somewhere?" Andrew swung Daniel up in his arms and perched him on his shoulders.

Forward.

The word stumbled recklessly out of her heart. Out of the laughter. And, for the first time, it felt like a good place to go.

Chapter Fourteen

He had to be dreaming. It was the only explanation. Bright afternoon sunlight flooded the tiny living room, unhampered by the heavy drapes that had covered the windows the last time he'd been there. Everything crafted from wood—from the floor beneath his feet to the trim on the old velvet couch—reflected a warm, satin glow. A large wicker hamper overflowing with children's books had taken over the spot where the ornate side table had been. The glass birds had been swept from the shelf to make room for the creamy rose that bowed gracefully in a slender, hand-painted vase.

Andrew knew he was staring at Miranda like an idiot but he couldn't help himself. The changes in the room weren't the only ones he noticed. The sound of Miranda's laughter had swept over him like a late summer coastal breeze. Light. Dazzling. Carrying the scent of change.

It was the last thing he'd expected to see when Daniel had opened the door.

Why was he always surprised when he went to a place and found God already there?

"We're painting my bedroom." Daniel broke the silence. "Do you want to help?"

"Daniel!" Miranda gasped. "I'm sure Andrew doesn't want to get paint all over his clothes."

She wouldn't look at him now. If she had, she would have noticed he wore a T-shirt and an ancient pair of blue jeans. The nicks and worn spots in the denim were real, not strategically placed there by a savvy designer.

"Let me guess—" Andrew directed his attention to Daniel, politely ignoring Miranda while she frantically stuffed clothing back into the suitcase "—you picked out the color…pink."

Daniel giggled. "No."

"Lavender."

"It's already that color."

It was? Somehow he'd missed that the night he'd tucked Daniel into bed. The room *had* been dark. The poor kid had lived with purple walls for four years? A sudden surge of hope jacked up his heart rate. Why was Miranda fixing up the apartment now? What had changed?

"It's *green.*" Daniel decided he'd made him guess long enough.

"Green." Andrew smacked his palm against his forehead. "Why didn't I think of that?"

The reward for his foolishness was another round of childish giggles. It reminded him of the chimes that rang in the bell tower of Chestnut Grove Community Church at noon every day. He never got tired of hearing them.

"If we're done by five o'clock, Mom's going to order pizza. From Gabriella's."

"Never let it be said that I turned down pizza from Gabriella's." Andrew winked at him.

"Sometimes you do," Miranda reminded him quietly.

Andrew absorbed the hit, knowing he deserved it. Over the last few days he'd struggled with the knowledge that he was asking Miranda to give him something he wasn't willing to give her. Trust. He'd tried to rationalize it with logic. If he told her what he did—who he was—there was a lot more at stake than a simple sharing of information. But even knowing that left him feeling like a hypocrite. Especially when he couldn't promise he wouldn't leave. Again. Without explanation.

He couldn't explain what brought him to their door on a Saturday morning. He'd stopped by the diner for breakfast and Sandra had casually mentioned Miranda had the weekend off.

After dropping Daniel off without a word a few days ago, Andrew had no idea if there would be a welcoming committee to meet him at the door. But he didn't care. He'd learned to recognize the nudge of the Spirit and that nudge told him to go to Miranda's.

And now he knew why.

He could help her finish what she'd started.

"The apartment looks…homey."

Miranda's face drained of color. Had he used the wrong word? Or the right one?

"Thank you." She rose to her feet and brushed off an invisible speck of dust from her knees. Once again Andrew absorbed her simple beauty. Even without makeup, her skin was flawless. The bandanna she'd used to pull her hair back only served to accentuate the classical lines of her face and gold-dust eyes.

But the laughter in those eyes was new.

"Come on, Andrew." Daniel bumped his heels against Andrew's sides as if he were a reluctant trail horse.

Andrew didn't move. He wouldn't stay unless Miranda invited him. He wouldn't push her and jeopardize the changes he saw. Or put shadows back in her eyes.

Miranda's shoulder lifted and fell. "You can see the paint Daniel picked out."

As far as invitations went, it didn't fall into the warm, cheery category. But it was a start.

He stepped around the suitcases, guided by the press of Daniel's hands on his shoulders.

"I'm just organizing things." Miranda must have seen his curious look.

He'd felt a stab of dread when he'd spotted the two suitcases on the floor and even though he knew there was more to the explanation than what Miranda was willing to share, his tension eased. He'd witnessed that airborne pair of socks. She'd been *unpacking* the suitcase.

Daniel's curtains were draped over a wooden chair in the corner, leaving his window bare, too. A drop cloth shrouded the bed, protecting it from drips. The room wasn't quite as barren as the living room but he noticed they didn't have much in the way of material possessions. Two bright yellow bins storing Daniel's toys stood in the closet and a microscope with a neat stack of slides was the centerpiece of the corner desk. A poster of the United States was tacked to the wall and a homemade mobile of the solar system swayed above his head, suspended by fishing line.

The only things on the nightstand next to Daniel's bed were a lamp shaped like an airplane and the baseball glove Andrew had given him. The lack of pictures in the house disturbed him. Even if Miranda and Daniel's father had divorced, it wouldn't be unusual for Daniel to have a photograph of his father in his bedroom. Not for the first time, he found himself wondering about the man who had captured Miranda's heart. And then broken it.

Andrew leaned over and Daniel slid down his arm.

"We're going to paint my bedroom first. And then the kitchen," Daniel said. "Maybe we'll even get a new stove. One that isn't from the Dark Ages. Right, Mom?"

"Daniel Thomas." Miranda slanted a meaningful look in his direction. "I'm sure Andrew doesn't want to hear all our plans."

Daniel ducked his head at the hint of exasperation in her voice. Andrew reached out and ruffled his hair.

"She used the dreaded middle name," he said solemnly. "You know what that means, don't you, sport?"

"I'm in trouble."

"*Almost* in trouble. First, middle and last means you're in trouble. Unless things have changed since I was your age."

Daniel's deep sigh was telling. "No. They haven't."

"I don't know if I like this." Miranda tried desperately not to smile. "It just occurred to me I'm outnumbered. Two against one."

That was because she hadn't figured out yet that he was on her side.

Andrew picked up a paintbrush. "It's two-thirty. That gives us two and a half hours to make our pizza deadline."

"No."

There was a moment of absolute silence in the room.

Daniel slid a worried glance at Andrew. "But, Mom—"

"No buts." She dipped it into the green paint and made an *O* on the wall. "We've got a game to finish first."

Daniel paused long enough to give Andrew an enthusiastic high five. Then he promptly beat her at tic-tac-toe.

Andrew tuned Daniel's clock radio to a station that played upbeat Christian music. Daniel began to hum along with one of the songs.

"We sang this one at Sonshine Camp," he told her. "Mrs. Fraser taught us lots of songs."

Andrew joined in, his smooth tenor raising goose bumps on her arms. It didn't make sense to her how Andrew could live a life of wasteful luxury and leave a trail of broken hearts while professing to follow Jesus. His faith seemed genuine, though, not the save-it-for-Sunday kind meant to impress people. It was almost as if Andrew was two different people. Or maybe he was like Hal. Pretending to be the kind of man she needed.

I don't need Andrew, she reminded herself. *And he certainly doesn't need me.*

When Andrew Noble finally decided to settle down, it would be with a woman as comfortable with wealth and privilege as he was. Someone who knew how to entertain important people. Someone who could drop everything on a moment's notice to fly to Paris. Someone like Samantha Harcourt.

Daniel and Andrew joined their voices enthusiastically in the chorus of the song. Daniel used his paintbrush as a drumstick against the side of the can while Andrew turned his into a conductor's baton.

She was amazed at how relaxed and content Daniel seemed to be in Andrew's company.

He needed a dad. But in order for that to happen, she needed a husband. And she wasn't sure if she'd ever be able to trust someone with her heart again.

Family.

Andrew knew he could get used to it. Even if it wasn't his.

He'd discovered early on that playing the role of wealthy vagabond, jet-setting on a moment's notice to exotic places, made people—like his curious cousin Rachel—less suspicious when he disappeared for days while searching for a missing child. He hadn't realized how starved his soul was for routine. For stability.

Daniel, spattered with paint, buzzed around the room like an energetic honeybee. Miranda occasionally took her brush and smoothed out a drip he'd forgotten. Never scolding. Never asking for a level of perfection a seven-year-old wasn't capable of.

She reminded him of his mom. Clara Noble had raised him the same way. With an inexhaustible well of patience and a box of Band-Aids always in reach. She hadn't skimped on hugs or a stern look when the occasion called for it. Clara had been there to calm his fears every time he'd relived the final hours of his abduction.

For months afterward, he'd woken up and found her asleep in the rocking chair in his bedroom, as if she'd sensed he might need her during the night.

Miranda was a bit overprotective but Daniel was blessed to have a mother who would be there for him, no matter what.

"Painting makes me hungry," Daniel announced. "If I eat a cookie, I'll still have room for pizza."

"Me, too." Andrew grinned down at Miranda from the top of the ladder.

"Men." Miranda rolled her eyes and put the paint-brush down. "I'll be right back."

Andrew hopped down from the ladder when she left the room. "Smart move, Danny boy."

Daniel flopped down on the braided rug, eager to take a break. A streak of green ran from his wrist to his elbow where he'd accidentally brushed against the wall. "I'm tired," he said with a heartfelt sigh. "Did you see my microscope? I got it for Christmas last year."

"It's a beauty." Andrew made a point of examining it more closely. "I had one of these when I was about your age."

"I have a book to go along with it. Want to see?" Daniel jumped up and opened the drawer of his nightstand. It was crammed with a small boy's treasures, which Daniel carefully removed and put on the bed.

A card snagged Andrew's attention. Obviously hand-made, the front featured a cartoon figure shaped like a ball. The glasses on the large brown eyes gave it away as to who it was supposed to be. Without thinking, he flipped it open to read the inscription.

To Daniel—my little Georgia Peach
Congratulations on First Place in the Science Fair!
Love, Mom

Daniel saw him reading it and wrinkled his nose. "That's what she calls me sometimes. It's silly, isn't it? I like *champ* better," he confided.

Andrew's gut tightened. He glanced at the door and heard Miranda still moving around in the kitchen.

"Why does she call you that?" he asked casually. "Did you used to live in Georgia?"

The sparkle in Daniel's eyes faded. He shrugged. "I don't know. Maybe."

"You don't remember moving to Chestnut Grove?"

Daniel looked down at the floor. "No." His voice dropped to a whisper. "But I remember the scary place."

Andrew stilled. "The scary place?"

"Mom thinks I don't remember it, but I do," Daniel said. "I think it was a scary place for her, too."

"What do you remember?" Andrew felt a twinge of guilt for prompting Daniel to answer his questions, but the lost look in Daniel's eyes unsettled him.

"I remember—"

"Daniel."

Andrew hadn't heard Miranda return but suddenly she was standing in the doorway behind them with a plate of cookies in her hand. Had she overheard their conversation?

Daniel bit his lip. "I wanted Andrew to see the microscope book."

Andrew scooped up the contents of the drawer and

gave them back to Daniel, careful to slip the card in without Miranda noticing.

He was more certain than ever that something had happened to put suspicion in Miranda's eyes. Something that cast shadows on Daniel's young memory.

The scary place.

Where was it? And what had happened there?

Turning her back so Andrew wouldn't notice the way her fingers trembled, Miranda set the plate of cookies down.

Daniel's words had shaken her to the core.

He'd never asked her about the past. Never, even out of childish curiosity. He had no memory of his parents but Miranda had explained the best she could that they were in heaven. It was important for him to know how much Lorraine and Tom had loved him, how they'd entrusted her to take care of him. For a few months after their deaths, Miranda had corrected Daniel when he'd called her Mama.

I'm Aunt Mandi, she'd reminded him, overwhelmed with guilt and feelings of inadequacy. Lorraine had been born to be a mother while Miranda had always been more career minded, pursuing her college degree and working her way up to loans manager at the bank.

Changing from the doting aunt who stopped by on the weekends with toys and treats to become the full-time mother of a toddler had left her reeling. And vulnerable.

With vivid clarity, she remembered the night she'd stopped insisting Daniel call her Aunt Mandi. An hour after she'd put him to bed in his crib, he'd started sobbing uncontrollably. Daniel's pediatrician had warned her Daniel would grieve his parents' death but would lack the words or ability to express his feelings. They would play out in the only way a two-year-old could express them. In tantrums or tears.

She'd gone into the bedroom and taken Daniel into her arms.

"Shh. Aunt Mandi's here," she murmured.

The tears hadn't stopped. If anything, the decibel level in the room increased.

No. Mama.

They clung together while hiccups punctuated Daniel's sobs. Miranda realized the difference between being an aunt and a mother was the ability to go back to her own life. Now, Daniel *was* her life.

"Mama's here, Daniel. Go to sleep."

As if her words had flipped an invisible switch, Daniel snuggled against her and closed his eyes.

A fierce rush of emotion swept through her. She hadn't given birth to Daniel. She felt totally unprepared for the task she'd been given but at that moment she knew this was what Lorraine would have wanted. Miranda wasn't Aunt Mandi anymore. In that moment, Daniel had truly become her son.

Miranda took a deep breath and slanted a look at Andrew. He and Daniel were trying to determine which cookie had the most chocolate chips. Maybe he'd interpret Daniel's mention of "the scary place" to a child's active imagination.

It unsettled her how quickly Daniel had formed an

attachment to a man who took pride in having no attachments. At least, for more than a day or two.

"Aren't you going to answer the phone, Mom?"

Andrew and Daniel were both staring at her now. She'd been so deep in thought she hadn't even heard it ring.

She returned moments later, a little dazed by the fact the call was for Daniel. She handed him the phone.

"For me?" Daniel grinned. He struck a casual pose that had both adults in the room trying not to laugh. "Hello?" He lowered the phone. "It's Olivia."

Miranda thought she'd recognized the voice.

"I think so. Let me ask my mom." Daniel's eyes shone. "She wants me to go to Sunday school with her in the morning. Her mom and dad will pick me up. She says you can come, too."

Red flags waved in Miranda's mind. Was that why Leah had offered to watch Daniel? Because she hoped to bring new recruits through the doors of Chestnut Grove Community Church?

"Tell Olivia you'll call her back after we've discussed it."

Daniel's face fell. The word *discussed* usually meant *no*. "But, Mom—"

"We'll talk about it later." When Andrew wasn't there.

"Okay." Daniel's gloomy voice reminded her of the donkey in the *Winnie the Pooh* cartoons they watched together. "Olivia? I probably can't go with you. My mom needs me to help her paint the kitchen tomorrow. Bye."

Guilt shot through Miranda as he handed the phone back to her. Lorraine and Tom had taken Daniel to church with them the first week they'd brought him home. Lorraine had insisted on keeping him with her through the entire service, too, never taking advantage of the well-staffed nursery. She'd told Miranda it was never too early to introduce a boy to the God who'd made him.

The only part of Lorraine's parenting philosophy Miranda had refused to embrace.

"Daniel, I—"

"It's okay. I forgot you needed my help." Daniel smiled at her and picked up his paintbrush again.

Another arrow of guilt pierced her. She felt Andrew's gaze but averted her eyes. She already felt exposed. He'd seen the suitcases. Heard Daniel talk about a scary place. And now he was up close and personal with her doubts and suspicions. She was surprised he didn't run screaming from the room.

"Leah is going to be my new babysitter," Daniel told Andrew. "Olivia has a playhouse and a sandbox with lots of trucks. The trucks are Joseph's but he's too little to play with them so he won't mind if I do."

Andrew glanced at her in surprise. "You asked Leah Cavanaugh to take care of Daniel?"

Miranda shook her head. "She called and offered." And now she had a hunch as to why.

Silence weighted the room for a moment.

"Leah is about as real as a person can get this side of heaven," Andrew said softly, as if she'd spoken her suspicions out loud.

Warm color tinted Miranda's cheeks. Andrew's quiet words reminded her that she'd always admired the young woman's warmth and bubbly personality. Leah wasn't the kind of person who had hidden motives or agendas.

Maybe suspicion was something else she needed to let go of. Like drapes that blocked out the sun. And suitcases buried in the back of the closet like time capsules.

"I think I can handle the kitchen by myself for a few hours tomorrow," she told Daniel. "Call Olivia back and find out what time they're going to pick you up."

"Really?" Daniel gave her an exuberant hug. Unfortunately, he forgot he had a paintbrush in his hand.

Miranda gasped.

"You better not sit down." Andrew barely suppressed a smile.

"I'll be right back." Miranda headed to her room to change clothes, absorbing the sound of Andrew and Daniel's laughter as it followed her out the door.

She'd gotten so used to Daniel's quiet play and the silence of her own company she'd forgotten how laughter could fill a room. Could make it come to life even more than a fresh coat of paint and new curtains.

Chapter Fifteen

Five minutes after Miranda sent Daniel off for church with the Cavanaughs the next morning, someone knocked on the door. Probably Mrs. Enderby, coming to check on her progress again.

The landlady had ignored her arthritic hip and tottered up to the apartment to see Daniel's bedroom just minutes after Andrew had left the day before. After one slice of pizza—and that was only because Daniel had challenged him to a race to see who could eat a piece the fastest—Andrew had glanced at his watch and told them he had an "appointment" and had to leave.

Miranda had read between the lines. It was Saturday night. A date night for someone who actually had a social life.

She'd said goodbye, trying to hide her disappointment.

What was wrong with her? Every time she decided she wasn't going to let Andrew Noble get close, he found a way to sneak under her defenses. Like showing up out of the blue and spending the afternoon painting Daniel's bedroom.

Mrs. Enderby—the Queen of Neutral Colors—had loved it. After inspecting Daniel's bedroom walls, she'd told Miranda she'd stop by to see the kitchen. Miranda hadn't expected it to be eight o'clock in the morning.

"Just a min…" Miranda opened the door and her voice faded into a gurgle.

Andrew stood on the landing, a white bakery box balanced in one hand and a carafe of fragrant coffee in the other. "I heard you could use a helper."

She saw the paintbrush sticking out of the pocket of his faded jeans and tried not to smile. "I thought you went to church."

"I'll go to the evening service tonight. Are you going to let me in to help or am I going to have to sit outside the window and torture you with the aroma of these double-chocolate-chip muffins?"

Miranda opened the door and let him into the apartment even as she recognized the truth.

Somehow, Andrew Noble had gotten into her heart.

"I don't know about you…" Andrew paused and rubbed the back of his neck, massaging away the dull ache that had taken up residence there. Payback for being a gentleman. He'd volunteered to paint the ceiling while Miranda had crouched on the floor, meticulously covering the scuffed baseboards with a fresh coat of Raspberry Mocha.

Once Miranda had gotten past her shock at seeing

him standing outside her front door, they'd worked in companionable silence for more than an hour.

"But I'm ready for a coffee break. And maybe another muffin."

Miranda smiled.

"What?" He wanted to know the thoughts that lay behind every one of those rare smiles. They reminded him of watching the sun peek through the clouds after a storm.

"You remind me of Daniel. I can't fill him up these days. I think he's grown two inches since school let out."

"I can't use that as an excuse. If I grow anywhere, it isn't going to be taller. It's going to be *wider*." Andrew patted his flat stomach.

"I don't think you have to worry…" Miranda's cheeks flooded with color and she looked away, embarrassed.

Andrew's eyebrow lifted. He thought blushing had gone out with cassette tapes. The women in the circles he traveled in wore their sophistication and experience like designer perfume.

Miranda's shy stammer caught him off guard. He wouldn't have expected it from a woman who'd been married and had a child.

"Why isn't Daniel back yet? I thought church ended at eleven." Miranda turned her back on him. Deliberately.

Andrew grinned.

"It is—"

As if on cue, the telephone rang.

"Hi, Leah." Miranda traced a finger along a jagged scratch on the kitchen table. "Lunch? I…suppose. No, two o'clock is fine. I know Daniel would love to go with you. Bye."

Miranda hung up the phone, looking as if she'd lost her best friend. Or realized her baby was growing up.

"Let me guess. You just got stood up by your favorite guy."

"It looks that way."

Could he be honest? At the risk of having the doors to Miranda's heart slam shut again?

Speak the truth in love.

Another bit of wisdom his mother would be proud to know he remembered.

"The Cavanaughs are good people, Miranda. They'll take care of Daniel."

"I know." Miranda forced a laugh. "But every time he's out of my sight…I just need to know he's safe. I sound silly."

"You sound like a mom," Andrew contradicted. "My mother took comfort in knowing that she couldn't always be with me but she knew God was. She'd say, 'I gave you to the Lord to hold, Andrew, and He hasn't dropped one of His children yet. I doubt you'll be the first.'"

Miranda forced a smile. "That sounds nice."

Andrew's frustration spiked. He could see in her eyes that she wanted to believe it. What held her back?

Patience, Andrew.

The same nudge that had brought him to Miranda's door the day before now cautioned him to back off. He listened. The changes he'd witnessed in Miranda's life over the past few weeks gave him hope. God was at work and the last thing Andrew wanted to do was get in the way.

"I'll take Daniel's place as your lunch date."

Miranda's eyes widened with panic. "No! I mean, I don't think you'd like what we were going to have."

"You think I'm a picky eater?"

"No, it's just that..." She rolled her eyes and gave a little huff. "When was the last time you ate a grilled-cheese sandwich?"

"I think I was ten."

"Exactly."

"Grilled-cheese sandwiches happened to be my favorite."

He waited, counting on Miranda's Southern gentility to override her reserve.

"It's processed American. The rubbery squares that come wrapped in plastic."

"Also my favorite." He managed to keep a straight face.

"You keep painting. I'll make the sandwiches."

Good manners won. He resisted the urge to whoop like Daniel had when he'd slid into home plate at the Fourth of July picnic. "Yes, ma'am." He drawled the words and saw a smile tug at her lips.

Thank you, Lord. You lead, I'll follow. Things always work out best that way.

Miranda dug into the fridge and pulled out the package of cheese. It almost slipped from her trembling hands.

Andrew Noble in her kitchen. On a ladder. Painting her ceiling.

Life couldn't get more surreal. Any moment, a camera crew would burst into her humble apartment and she'd find out she was the unwitting star of some crazy new television show.

The flipside of that nightmare was being alone with him. Sitting across from each other eating grilled-cheese sandwiches.

The camera crew looked better and better.

She enjoyed Andrew's company way too much for her peace of mind. His sense of humor coaxed laughter from a place inside her that she thought life had completely emptied. He kept his distance, never crowding her. Even when he turned on that legendary Noble charm, she sensed a depth and sincerity in him that most people seemed to overlook.

One word came to mind when she thought of Andrew.

Dangerous.

Fumbling with the loaf of bread, she concentrated on making the most perfect grilled-cheese sandwiches ever to grace the skillet on Mrs. Enderby's temperamental old stove.

"You look like you've got this down to a science." Andrew jumped down from the ladder and edged closer to watch.

Miranda nodded. Hopefully her ability to speak would return. When the tangy scent of his cologne wasn't teasing her senses.

Rattled by his closeness, Miranda deposited the sandwiches on the griddle and stepped away. Right onto the wooden stick she'd used to stir the paint. It attached itself to the bottom of her shoe like a wad of chewing gum.

Miranda teetered as she lifted her foot to pull it off and grabbed on to the only solid thing in the vicinity.

Andrew's shoulder.

She yanked the stick away and dropped it on the

newspaper. Raspberry Mocha paint dripped from the sole of her shoe. Still holding on to Andrew for balance, she peeled off her tennis shoe, too.

The smell of burning grilled-cheese sandwiches filled the air.

Miranda groaned.

"They're burning…" Her voice died in her throat.

Andrew's arms had come around her to steady her and when she tried to wiggle away to rescue their lunch, he didn't let her go. Green and gold fire danced in his eyes, reminding her of pictures she'd seen of the northern lights.

"Miranda?" The question in his husky voice made her heart skip a beat. The pad of his thumb traced her jaw and came to rest on the pulse beating wildly in her throat.

He wanted to kiss her. But he wouldn't without her permission. In that moment, Miranda knew everything she'd heard and read about Andrew Noble was wrong. No matter what evidence existed to the contrary, he wasn't the kind of man who carelessly played with women's hearts and tossed them aside.

Yes.

She didn't say the word aloud but he read it in her eyes. A half a step brought them closer. He gathered her against him and lowered his head, his lips gentle and searching. He didn't demand a response; he coaxed one from her.

With one kiss, Andrew wiped away the memory of Hal's rough embraces.

Head over heels.

For the first time, Andrew knew what it meant.

The gentle press of Miranda's hands against his back and her tentative response turned him inside out. Totally shaken, he released her.

"I'm sorry, Miranda." Still feeling the aftershock of that kiss, he took a step back and shoved his hands into his pockets. The bewildered look in her eyes made him want to tug her right back into his arms. "I didn't mean for that to happen."

"Neither did I." Miranda's fingers touched her lips.

He'd ruined it. Now she'd look for strings attached to his offer of friendship. Miranda would assume she'd just become another number in Andrew Noble's little black book....

"But I don't think I'm sorry." She blushed right after she said the words, as if she hadn't meant to speak them out loud.

Andrew stared at her.

The hiss of the skillet, a small cloud of black smoke and the unexpected shriek of the smoke detector brought both of them back to reality.

Miranda grabbed a pot holder and lunged toward the oven but Andrew plucked it out of her hand.

"No way. This is my knight-in-shining-armor moment when I rescue the fair maiden from terror and certain death...."

Miranda had the skillet in the sink and the window open by the time he finished his monologue.

"Let's try that again." Miranda sighed, dumping the soggy remains of their lunch into the garbage.

"Are you talking about the sandwiches?" Andrew grinned.

Miranda blushed. Again.

Andrew resisted the urge to kiss her. Again.

"Let me run out and get something at the deli." He needed to put some distance between them so he could think straight. And pray. And ask God to forgive him for his stupidity. He'd jeopardized the fragile trust Miranda had offered by inviting him into her home. And her life.

"You don't have to—"

Yes, he did.

"You wouldn't let me rescue you from the evil skillet. At least let me buy you lunch." Andrew escaped before Miranda could finish her halfhearted protest.

When the door closed, Miranda sagged against the counter and closed her eyes. She didn't know how to begin to sort through the tangle of emotions Andrew's kiss had created.

Miranda knew Hal had somehow damaged her soul the day he'd pushed her against the wall. She'd trusted him and he'd betrayed her. His aggressive show of strength had left bruises not only on the outside but on the inside, too.

She'd kept men at a wary distance ever since then. At the diner, if one of them somehow managed to edge into her personal space, she felt smothered. Trapped. At times Miranda wondered if she could ever trust a man to get close to her again without feeling that overwhelming sense of panic.

She hadn't felt that way with Andrew.

Maybe because he'd asked instead of demanded. Given more than he'd taken.

I don't think I'm sorry.

Miranda's cheeks heated as she remembered the reckless words that had spilled out. Instead of using her honesty to his advantage, his tender smile and gentle humor had given her back her dignity.

Daniel was right.

Andrew *was* one of the good guys.

The Cavanaughs' dark green SUV pulled alongside the curb as Andrew parked his own car in Miranda's narrow driveway.

Daniel and Olivia tumbled out of the backseat and Daniel made a beeline for him.

"Did you come to see me?" Daniel raised his arms, eager to reclaim his perch on Andrew's shoulders.

"I came to help your mom paint the kitchen." Andrew looped the grocery bag around his wrist and hoisted Daniel up. Olivia giggled as she watched them.

Andrew walked over to the window to say hello to Ben and Leah and saw Joseph sleeping peacefully in his car seat.

"Can you come up and say hello? I couldn't decide between raspberry cordial and death by chocolate cheesecake. So I bought them both."

Leah smiled but the serious set of Ben's jaw didn't ease.

Andrew put Daniel down and handed him the bag. "Will you and Olivia run this upstairs for me, champ? And tell your mom I'll be right there."

"Okay." Daniel tugged on Olivia's hand. "You can see my room."

Andrew waited until they disappeared. He hadn't spoken to Rachel in a few days but the Lord continually brought the Cavanaugh family to mind during Andrew's prayer time. He'd been a believer long enough to know that was never a coincidence. "Is everything all right?"

"I talked to Reverend Fraser after church this morning. I've decided to call the Watsons when we get home." Ben laughed softly. "To tell you the truth, I haven't been this nervous since I asked Leah to marry me."

"And I couldn't resist you." Leah gave her husband's shoulder an affectionate squeeze. "I doubt the Watsons will be able to, either."

"Let me know how it goes," Andrew said. "I'll be praying for you."

"We will," Leah promised.

Andrew took a few steps and paused. "Thanks for taking Daniel to church and out to lunch."

"Don't thank us. Daniel is a real sweetie. Easy to love."

Andrew glanced up and saw Miranda framed in the window.

So is his mother.

He didn't say the words out loud but when he caught a glimpse of Leah's knowing smile, he knew he might as well have.

Chapter Sixteen

Ross stirred the stacks of papers on his desk and wondered why God had handpicked him to be the bearer of bad news.

"It's a good thing *killing the messenger* isn't a viable option, anymore, Lord," Ross muttered, staring at the name penciled in the square on his calendar.

Ben Cavanaugh. He was on a job site with Jonah in Richmond and couldn't meet with Ross until later that afternoon.

As soon as Kelly had called him with the latest news, he'd been burdened with guilt. Ben had mustered the courage to phone the Watsons the day before and had discovered the tragic news.

Millicent Cunningham Watson—Ben's biological mother—had passed away several years ago.

Ross blamed himself. He'd been too anxious to share the initial information about Ben's birth mother. He should have waited and checked further into the family before giving Ben the Watsons' telephone number.

Finding out he had four adult half siblings and that Millicent and Ralph had searched for him, too, couldn't completely erase Ben's grief over losing the opportunity to meet the woman who'd brought him into the world.

Would Ben still want to meet the family? Knowing his birth mother had passed away? It had taken Ben a long time to make the decision to find her and now he had another difficult decision to make.

Ross shifted restlessly in the chair. He had to apologize to Ben as soon as possible for dropping the ball. His concern about Kelly and the threatening note had drummed out everything else in his brain lately. Not that it was a valid excuse, but he hoped Ben would understand.

A rap on the door interrupted his thoughts.

"Come in."

He already knew who was on the other side. Appointment Number Two. Andrew Noble. It was a good thing that nothing fazed the guy because this meeting had the potential to be a rough one, too.

Lord, whenever you say the word, I'm ready to retire.

He motioned to Andrew to sit down.

In a split second, Andrew decided he'd rather stand. The guarded expression on Ross's face didn't exactly invoke a warm, fuzzy make-yourself-at-home type of feeling.

Ross opened his mouth to say something and then his jaw snapped shut again.

Andrew strolled in and lounged against the wall but every nerve ending in his body was on red alert. The P.I.

didn't strike Andrew as the kind of man who had a difficult time saying what was on his mind.

Ross fixed his gaze on the pictures of the children that lined the wall above the desk. As if he'd forgotten Andrew was still in the room.

A sudden, chilling thought occurred to Andrew. Had Ross somehow stumbled upon the fact that Andrew was the Guardian?

"Is Kelly all right?" He decided to jumpstart the conversation by turning Ross's thoughts to his wife.

"Kelly?" Ross gave him a distracted look, which sharpened when he realized he'd been caught daydreaming. The reddish haze in his eyes testified to the hours he'd put in chasing paper trails. "She's fine."

And she's going to stay that way.

Andrew heard the unspoken words and waited. So Ross's phone call wasn't about the threatening letter Kelly had received.

"This thing is like mountain climbing," Ross murmured, almost to himself. "Every time I think I have a hold on something, the rocks under my feet start to crumble."

Andrew could relate to that. No matter how difficult, you couldn't go back. Only forward. "Is there anything I can do?"

Ross barely concealed his surprise. And his amusement. "Thanks for the offer, but I can't think of anything."

Andrew almost smiled. The guy was tactful, no doubt about it.

"Jared Kierney, Meg's husband, is helping with damage control. He got permission from his editor at the

Gazette to write a special series of articles about Tiny Blessings. He's planning to interview the Harcourts first. Give a more personal spin on adoption to counter the bad press the agency's been dealing with."

"It should help." Andrew crossed his arms loosely over his chest, adopting the casual stance that encouraged people to let their guard down. To underestimate him. If Ross knew his secret, he would have said so by now. Something else was going on....

Ross gave him a level look. "What do you know about Miranda Jones?"

The question broadsided him. Tension cinched the muscles in his shoulders, pulling him out of his casual slouch. "Is there a reason you think I should know something about her?"

Ross flicked an impatient look at him. "Don't play games with me, Noble. I'm not the press or a member of your fan club. Sandra is like a second mother to me and since the incident at the Fourth of July celebration, Kelly now claims Miranda as a friend. Those are the two reasons I called you...first. So, at the risk of repeating myself...what do you know about Miranda?"

Right before Ross's eyes, Andrew Noble shed the facade of pampered American prince. His gaze was sharp and alert. "And at the risk of repeating *myself,* what makes you think I know anything?"

Respect flickered in Ross's eyes. "Kelly seems to think you and Miranda are seeing each other. Although, she did admit Miranda denied it."

"We've been spending time together," Andrew said, not entirely surprised his friendship with Miranda had become a topic of conversation. Curiosity overrode caution and he decided to answer Ross's questions. "She's a loyal employee. A devoted mother." He started with the things he knew were true and left out the blanks he'd been trying to fill as he got to know Miranda better.

"Devoted?" Ross picked up on the word immediately. His fingers drummed an uneven beat against the top of the desk. "How devoted?" he muttered. "That's the question."

On the outside, Andrew appeared to be the kind of man accustomed to having everything he wanted at the snap of his fingers, but years of working as the Guardian had carved out a reservoir of patience. Until now.

His eyes narrowed. "What are you getting at?"

"I wish I knew." Ross pushed a thin sheaf of papers across the desk. "Take a look."

For a second, Andrew didn't move. Didn't want to see what was in the harmless-looking papers that had prompted Ross's phone call. And how they connected to Miranda. The only thing that kept one foot in front of the other as he stalked over to the desk was the knowledge that God walked with him.

He scanned the letterhead at the top of the page. They were adoption papers.

"What—" It was typical legalese. Nothing in the endless flow of words snagged his attention. Until Ross leaned forward and flipped the page.

"Keep reading."

Andrew's vision blurred.

The names of the adoptive parents, a Lorraine and Thomas Ferris from Atlanta, Georgia, didn't mean anything to him. But the signature of the witness did.

Miranda Lynn Jones.

And the name of the adoptive child.

Daniel Thomas Ferris.

"This has to be a coincidence. The names…a lot of people share the same name." Questions boiled over in his mind.

If Daniel was adopted, where were his parents? And why was Miranda claiming to be Daniel's *mother.*

"I talked to Sandra after I found these yesterday afternoon. They were with some other documents sealed in a separate envelope in the strong box. I haven't had a chance to examine them closely yet. They don't look like they were tampered with but the deeper Harcourt got into blackmailing people, the better he got at falsifying documents." Ross hesitated. "Sandra doesn't know what to think. When Miranda applied for the job at the diner, she got the impression Miranda was afraid of something. Or someone. She assumed Miranda had had a bad breakup with Daniel's father. Miranda told her Daniel was her son and Sandra never questioned it. My mother-in-law has a habit of reaching out to lost souls. She hired Miranda on the spot without asking for references. She did verify Daniel's birth date as the one listed here on the adoption papers. They're the same."

Another coincidence?

Andrew tried to piece together his fractured thoughts. "This doesn't make sense. You're telling me that Daniel Jones was adopted? Through Tiny Blessings?"

"According to these papers, it appears that way. But why were they hidden in a wall at the mansion?" Ross posed the question but judging from his tone, he'd already formed a theory about that. Barnaby Harcourt had taken his blackmail very seriously. He hadn't simply run out of space in his filing cabinet. He'd put the documents there for a reason.

Like a flash flood, conversations Andrew'd had with Miranda slammed into him. The look of fear on her face when she'd overheard his conversation with Sandra about the newly discovered cache of documents. Her vague responses to his questions about where she'd lived before moving to Chestnut Grove. The way she'd kept to herself, gently rebuffing any attempts people made to befriend her. To let anyone get to know her. Everything pointed to one conclusion.

A woman on the run.

"Sandra asked me to call you," Ross went on. "She warned me not to jump to conclusions and she's afraid if I approach Miranda, she'll take Daniel and leave."

The suitcases…

Andrew's heart kicked into an unsteady rhythm. "You want me to talk to her."

"Sandra says Miranda trusts you."

Apparently not enough, Andrew thought bitterly. If he believed the documents in front of him, Miranda had only been a witness to Daniel's adoption. She wasn't his birth mother. Or even his adoptive mother.

So, who was she?

His thoughts took a dark turn. Was it possible Miranda had somehow been involved in one of Harcourt's blackmailing schemes?

"If you don't feel comfortable talking to Miranda, I'll keep digging," Ross said quietly. "But I have to be honest. Finding out who's responsible for sending Kelly that note is my top priority at the moment."

Andrew didn't blame him. He felt the same overpowering need to protect Miranda. Despite the evidence, he wanted to believe there was a logical explanation why Miranda and Daniel were together.

"She loves him."

He didn't realize he'd said the words out loud until Ross clamped a bracing hand on his shoulder. "I'm sure she does. But sometimes people act out of a misguided sense of what's right."

It was true. In the past, Andrew had searched for children who'd been abducted by noncustodial parents. When the children were found, some of the parents were stunned they were being arrested for "abducting" their child. They insisted they were "rescuing" them.

Was it really possible Miranda had abducted Daniel? A sick feeling spread through him like a cancer, eating away at his peace of mind. Making him doubt.

He remembered what it had felt like to be taken from away from his family. The rough hands that had urged him into the damp basement. The heavy footsteps pacing over his head. The eyes burning with hostility behind the slits in the mask his abductor had worn. The shootout with the police that had resulted in the death of the man who'd taken him from his family.

No matter what the situation—stranger or noncustodial parent—a missing child was a frightened child. A child who needed to be found and brought back home.

Was Daniel one of those children?

Everything inside him rebelled against it.

God, help me find out the truth. I know You've been working in Miranda's life. Your word promises You'll work all things together for good for those who love You. You know I love You and I trust You. No matter what happens, draw Miranda to You. Show her that You are faithful. That You love her.

The truth crashed over him. His feelings for Miranda may have been rooted in friendship but at some point in time, she'd worked her way into his heart.

He loved her, too.

Miranda parked her car in front of the Cavanaughs' home and quickly plucked out the tiny shard of envy that lodged in her heart at the sight of the spacious lawn surrounding the older, well-kept home. The kind of home she wanted for Daniel. Warm and welcoming. The lush grass was neatly trimmed and flowers bordered the stone foundation of the house, a cheerful explosion of color as unique as the clothing Leah wore. A pink playhouse built to resemble a whimsical miniature castle nestled in the comforting shade of an ancient oak.

Daniel and Olivia careened around the side of the house, a shaggy dog the size of a bear cub loping along behind them.

"Mom!" Daniel veered off course and met her on the cobbled sidewalk. "Can we stay longer?"

"Please," Olivia chimed in.

"You've been here all morning." Miranda hugged him hard and smiled at Olivia. "I take it you two had fun."

Both heads bobbed vigorously.

"This is Bear." Olivia grabbed the dog's leather collar

just before he bowled Miranda over. "Dad says Bear thinks he's a Chihuahua."

The dog groaned contentedly when Miranda reached down to scratch his ear. "Where is your mom?"

"She's in the kitchen making peanut-butter cookies." Olivia lowered her voice to a whisper. "If you go inside, you have to be quiet. Joseph is taking a nap."

"I will," Miranda promised. "You have exactly five minutes. You better make the most of them." She winked at Olivia. "Daniel will be back tomorrow morning."

"Daniel told me you're a nice mom," Olivia said with a grin. She grabbed his hand and they raced to the playhouse.

Unexpected tears stung Miranda's eyes as the sound of their laughter bubbled out of the castle.

"I'm trying, Lorraine," she whispered. "I know the only thing you and Thomas wanted was to raise Daniel. And you probably wouldn't have made the mistakes I've made. But no one could love Daniel as much as I do. And I promise I'll stop looking over my shoulder and I'll concentrate on making a home for him. He'll have good friends like Olivia and I'll let him play baseball. And I'll…I'll take him to church because I know that's what you would have wanted."

Without realizing it, the words had carried her up the path to the front door. Where Leah waited.

"Can you stay for a cup of coffee? I'll bring it to *you* for a change."

Miranda hesitated, knowing Daniel and Olivia would be thrilled with a few extra minutes to play.

"Peanut-butter cookies, fresh from the oven?"

"A bribe?" Miranda was only half joking.

"I prefer to call it an *incentive.*" Leah's smile was mischievous as she motioned for Miranda to follow her inside.

The handcrafted oak table was a worthy centerpiece in the large kitchen that reflected the cozy atmosphere of the rest of the home. Just like in Miranda's own kitchen, Leah had filled a canning jar with fresh flowers. Breezy muslin valances framed the large window over the sink and a collection of Olivia's artwork graced the sunny yellow walls.

"An incentive." Miranda perched on the edge of one of the chairs, reluctant to get too comfortable. "I'm going to have to remember that when I'm trying to get Daniel to eat something other than macaroni and cheese for lunch."

"No one said parenting is easy." Leah poured two cups of coffee and sat down opposite Miranda at the table. "Olivia was already seven when Ben and I got married. I may have been a nanny, but I had a lot of catching up to do when it came to being a mom."

"So did—" Miranda pressed her lips together, horrified she'd almost said the words out loud. *So did I.* Exactly why she found it safer to keep her distance from people. When she let her guard down, bits and pieces of her past could escape.

Leah continued as if Miranda hadn't snapped off the end of her sentence. "The hardest thing was discipline. Olivia would flash those puppy-dog eyes at me and I'd say yes to just about anything."

Daniel's soulful brown eyes came instantly to mind. "I know exactly what you mean."

Leah raised her coffee cup. "To mothers. All for one and one for all."

"Didn't the three musketeers say that?"

"Yes, but I'm sure they heard it from their mothers first." Leah grinned.

Miranda raised her hand and the two cups clinked together.

As if on cue, the baby monitor on the kitchen counter crackled and they heard Joseph coo.

"Excuse me, friend." Leah paused just long enough to slide some cookies onto a plate and deposit them in front of Miranda. "I'll be back in a few minutes."

Friend.

A few weeks ago, that word and the expectations attached to it would have made Miranda bolt for the door the second Leah left the room. She didn't need friends. Hadn't wanted them. Five minutes in Leah's company and she'd almost blurted out something guaranteed to stir Leah's curiosity. Raise questions Miranda couldn't answer.

So why are you still here?

The quiet voice that invaded her thoughts encouraged honesty. Miranda shifted in the chair.

Because Daniel needs friends.

She offered up the logical answer and her heart immediately rejected it. It was getting harder to keep it in line, as if it were no longer willing to stay imprisoned by the past.

Maybe I need friends, too.

The softly spoken words didn't just spill over the walls she'd spent years erecting, they wiped them out.

She found more freedom in the truth than in her halfhearted attempts to rationalize her fears. And if she followed this new feeling to its source, she knew exactly who she'd find there. God.

Was it possible He was still there? That maybe He'd never left her at all?

Stunned by the revelation, Miranda didn't hear Leah approach until she appeared in the doorway with Joseph in her arms.

"I wish I could nap in the afternoons," Leah said as she sank into the chair. "I'd wake up all bright eyed and bushy tailed like this little guy."

Joseph did look alert. His eyes tracked his mother's voice to her face and he grinned up at her.

"Is he still waking up a lot during the night?"

Leah shook her head. "I was up a lot last night but I can't blame Joseph. I was praying for Ben." Leah hesitated and a shadow swept across her face. "Sandra might have mentioned that Ross found Ben's birth mother. Yesterday he called the number Ross had given him and found out she passed away several years ago."

"I'm sorry." The words sounded small to Miranda's ears. "That must have been hard."

"It was," Leah agreed. "But it helps to know our friends are praying for us. And to know that God loves us. God never wastes our pain or our tears. We might not understand the reasons why we go through hard times, but we choose to trust He'll ultimately use them for His glory."

Miranda wove her fingers together in her lap to keep them from shaking.

If she offered God the fragments of her heart…the pain of her past…could He really make something new?

What had Sandra said? Something about God exchanging beauty for ashes?

The words echoed in Miranda's heart.

I think I'm ready for beauty, God.

Chapter Seventeen

A soft light glowed inside the diner, backlighting Miranda's silhouette as she leaned over the paperwork on the table.

Andrew rapped lightly on the window and saw her start of surprise as she turned in his direction.

And smiled when she recognized him.

The first natural smile she'd ever given him. Freely given without a hint of suspicion. Or fear. The smile he'd been waiting—hoping for—from the first moment he'd seen her.

Why now, God?

Miranda fumbled with the lock and opened the door without hesitation, her gaze lighting on the cluster of miniature rosebuds in his hand. The shy tilt of her lips almost wrecked him.

"Have you had dinner yet?" He knew she hadn't.

"I work in a diner." The golden shower of sparks in her eyes glowed with a warmth that stole his breath.

Miranda Jones was teasing him. Something much riskier than a smile. He swallowed. Hard.

"But you've never tasted my famous lobster Newburg." She didn't have to know it was compliments of one of Rachel's friends who owned a catering business in Richmond.

Miranda stilled. "You're inviting me over for dinner?"

"Everything's ready. The only thing missing is...you."

She fingered the fragile petals of the roses. "I was just finishing up."

He knew that. He'd timed it that way. And even though he also knew the answer to his next question, he asked it anyway. "Where is Daniel tonight?"

"He's with Darcy. She begged me to let her take him to a movie. It's animated. She had to borrow a child so she wouldn't feel silly. They're going out for ice cream after it's over. I have about an hour and a half."

"Is that a yes?" A week ago, he would have traded in his Porsche for a rusty pickup truck to get her to agree to a dinner date. But not now. Not when he knew what the topic of conversation was going to be.

Are you really Daniel's mother or did you steal him?

Miranda nodded. "It's a yes."

Fifteen minutes later, Miranda sat in his car, cradling the roses in her hands, as he drove to the renovated upscale area near the James River where Rachel's loft was located.

"Did Daniel enjoy his first day at the Cavanaughs'?" The last thing Andrew wanted to do was make small talk. His gut tightened the closer they got to the apartment complex.

"He can't wait to go back tomorrow morning. Ben

built a playhouse for Olivia last summer and it was all he could talk about. According to Daniel, there's even electricity in it."

Andrew heard the wistful thread in her voice and knew Miranda would give her son the world if she could.

None of this makes sense, Lord.

His thoughts replayed a familiar litany. Harcourt had somehow messed up Daniel's paperwork. Daniel and Miranda looked alike. The bond between them was real. Miranda's reserve had to be the fallout from a nasty divorce. Anything but what the evidence pointed to. That Miranda was a woman on the run with a child who wasn't hers.

He took advantage of the valet parking. Every second counted. He nodded to the security guard, who opened the doors and gave Miranda a respectful nod.

Out of the corner of his eye, Andrew saw Miranda's expression as she took in the spacious foyer. The developer who'd converted the six-story warehouse into condominiums had preserved the crisp but elegant lines of the original building and accentuated them with dramatic combinations of black and white.

"This is beautiful." Miranda peered at her reflection in the marble floor as they walked to the elevator.

"Rachel kept the apartment after she married Eli so she could offer it to people who needed a place to stay. The last couple who lived here were missionaries from Bolivia. At the moment, it's my turn." Andrew wondered fleetingly if Miranda would like his house in Rhode Island. It had been constructed on a secluded ridge of rocky beach years before zoning restrictions existed. The waves practically kissed the stone foundation. The wooden floors were scuffed, the comfortable furniture an eclectic blend of estate-sale relics. An abundance of windows captured the changing faces of the ocean. He traveled all over the world but it was the place he considered home. It was also the place he wanted to raise a family someday….

Miranda read between the lines. Rachel's loft was temporary, just like his job overseeing the Noble Foundation. He couldn't have made it any clearer. A man as wealthy as Andrew probably owned too many houses to call any of them home.

For at least the tenth time since they'd left the diner she wondered why she'd agreed to have dinner with him. Alone. It was crazy. Maybe she should *serve* him his dinner and go home….

Distracted by her thoughts, she'd hardly been aware of stepping into the elevator. When the door silently opened on the fifth floor, she followed Andrew to the end of the hall. He unlocked the door to the apartment and stepped to the side so she could go in first.

A tiny gasp caught in her throat. The last time she'd seen a great room similar to the one in Rachel's apartment, she'd been paging through a home decorating magazine in the waiting room at the doctor's office.

Skylights in the vaulted ceiling framed the stars against a backdrop of black velvet sky. A wall of glass overlooked the river five stories below, where antique lampposts illuminated a walkway through the parklike lawn.

Gleaming chrome-and-glass furnishings were softened by a collection of personal keepsakes from

Rachel's travels abroad. Classical music drifted from a hidden sound system somewhere in the walls.

"Rachel loves to decorate. Cooking, not so much." Andrew's hand touched the small of her back as he ushered her farther into the room. The warmth of his fingers burned through the thin cotton fabric of her shirt and sent chills up both arms. The contradictory sensation was as confusing as her feelings for him.

This wasn't a good idea.

"Are you cold?" Andrew noticed the raised bumps on her bare arms.

"It must be the air-conditioning."

"It's on the lowest setting." Andrew's fingers skimmed a path down her arms. Wonderful. Now she had goose bumps on top of goose bumps.

She pulled the ragged edges of her heart together and forced a smile. "Let me help you with dinner."

Andrew didn't smile back.

Miranda suddenly felt chilled and it had nothing to do with the air conditioner.

She followed Andrew into a gourmet kitchen that would turn Isaac green with envy. For someone who didn't enjoy cooking, Rachel had still invested in top-of-the-line appliances. One piece of the cookware artistically hanging from the decorative iron rack above their heads cost more than a week's salary at the diner.

Andrew stopped so abruptly Miranda almost bumped into him. "Everything is ready. All I have to do is set the table."

"Let me do something," Miranda offered with a

smile, still unsure of his strange mood. "I'm not used to being waited on."

"Here." He plucked a ladle out of a crock stuffed with cooking utensils. "You can dish up while I cut the bread and set the table."

The lobster Newburg looked delicious. Miranda's nose twitched appreciatively as she transferred it from the pot to the heavy stoneware tureen and carried it into the formal dining room.

He'd set the table for two. Delicate cream-colored plates trimmed in gold. Crystal water goblets. Linen napkins.

She'd never been treated to an evening like this before.

"Should we light the candles?"

Andrew hesitated long enough to draw that uneasy shiver back to the surface. What was going on?

"Sure."

The trio of chunky candles cast a warm glow over the table and Miranda pulled one of the upholstered chairs away from the table. Andrew stepped behind her, his hand resting on the back of her chair.

She waited for him to push it in. And waited. When she glanced up, it was to find him staring down at her with an unreadable expression on his face.

"Is something wrong?" she finally gathered up the courage to ask.

"I can't do this."

Miranda's mouth dried up. She couldn't even ask the question hammering to get out. *Can't do what?*

Andrew jerked another chair away from the table and he sat down, his eyes piercing her with their intensity.

"I care about you, Miranda. I care about Daniel, too. Do you believe me?"

Stunned, Miranda managed to nod. She did believe him. He'd proven it in dozens of ways over the past few weeks. It didn't make it any less surreal, though. She was a waitress at the Starlight Diner. A single mother who cut coupons and walked to work to save money on gasoline.

"I—"

Andrew reached out and pressed two fingers gently against her lips, preventing her from telling him she felt the same way. "I talked to Ross this morning, Miranda. He found Daniel's adoption papers mixed in with the ones Jonah found at the mansion."

A cold trickle of fear skittered through her. Numbed her. She jumped to her feet and stumbled blindly toward the door.

Andrew blocked her path.

Her heart pounded in her chest.

This isn't Hal. It's Andrew.

The frantic reminder didn't calm the surge of fear that choked her. She tried to skirt around him but he caught her hand.

"Talk to me, Miranda. Daniel's parents are listed as Lorraine and Tom Ferris. You witnessed the documents but you're claiming to be Daniel's mother. Why?"

Her worst nightmare had come to life. Except in her worst nightmare, her accuser wasn't the man she'd been foolish enough to fall in love with.

"I know Lorraine and Tom Ferris died. Was Daniel going to be put into foster care? Did you take him away from someone who wasn't treating him well? I want to help you, Miranda, but I can't unless you're honest with me."

Horrified, it dawned on her what Andrew was implying. "You think I *abducted* Daniel?"

She could see it in his eyes. He'd already judged her and found her guilty. The tiny shoots of hope that had sprung up over the past few days withered and died. Crushed by the weight of his accusations.

"I don't know what to think." Frustration roughened Andrew's voice. "You won't tell people about your past. You don't let anyone get close. Daniel told me he remembers living in a scary place before you came to Chestnut Grove."

The color drained from Miranda's face.

"What did he mean, Miranda? Trust me—"

"Trust you?" The words burst out of her as the truth began to sink in. He'd manipulated her. From the moment he'd appeared at the diner with a handful of roses and a dinner invitation. She'd let her guard down and he'd taken advantage of it. "You planned this whole evening. This is why you brought me here, isn't it? To accuse me of…" She couldn't even say the words.

The one man she'd let slip through her defenses believed she was capable of a…crime. A crime involving the child she'd done everything in her power to love and protect.

The worst part was that some tiny seed of hope refused to die. She wanted—needed—him to deny it. He didn't.

"I had to talk to you alone." Andrew's voice gentled. "I want to hear your side of the story. I want to help you."

"No." She shook her head and backed away from him while a voice inside her head mocked her for believing in candlelight and music. For believing in Andrew.

She'd thought she could hide from the past but she'd been wrong. She'd let herself dream she could build a new future but she'd been wrong about that, too. She'd been wrong about everything. About everyone. Even about God. If He cared about her, she wouldn't be going through this.

She was on her own. Again.

Andrew saw the change in her expression. Resignation extinguished the anger in her eyes.

"I don't *need* your help." Her voice was so low he had to strain to hear her. "Lorraine Ferris was my sister. She and her husband, Tom, were killed by a drunk driver when Daniel was two. Daniel was adopted from Tiny Blessings but in their will, they'd named me as his legal guardian if anything happened to them. We lived in another state and I petitioned for adoption. It's what my sister wanted—she trusted me to take care of Daniel. To protect him."

"To protect him from who? Harcourt?"

A shudder ripped through her but she flinched when he reached out to her. Andrew let his arms drop to his sides. By trying to help, he'd made things worse. Just when she'd started to trust him, he'd proven he didn't trust *her.*

"Miranda, let's get to the bottom of this. Together. Harcourt stashed Daniel's adoption papers in the mansion. It's possible his adoption wasn't legal—"

Panic flared in Miranda's eyes. "I'm leaving."

Leaving Chestnut Grove. She didn't have to say it. Emotion was driving her now. She wasn't going to lose her son. He'd let his own demons from the past and his fear he'd lose Miranda take over. He'd pushed her too hard, too fast.

"Don't run away. I can help, Miranda. There's something I haven't told you—"

"I don't want to hear it." Her eyes were flat. Lifeless. "And I don't want to…see you again. Stay away from me. And Daniel."

"Miranda." He wanted to wrap his arms around her and make her stay until they'd worked everything out. But eventually he'd have to let her go. There was only one thing that would keep Miranda from taking Daniel and running again.

She had to feel safe.

And there was only one place she could run where she would be completely safe. The same place he'd discovered when he was five years old.

Show her, Lord. Show her it's You.

It took all of Miranda's self-control not to run down the long hall and out of the building. She reached the doors and the security guard stepped in front of her.

"Miss Jones? Could you please wait here for a moment?"

For a heart-stopping second, she thought Andrew had decided to keep her there until the police arrived and questioned her.

"Mr. Noble called for a car to take you home."

"I…" She had no choice. She had ten dollars in her

purse, which wouldn't cover the cost of a taxi home. "Thank you."

The guard lifted his arm to signal the car that rounded the corner of the building. A limousine. The sight of the gleaming vehicle was like salt in an open wound. A reminder that Andrew Noble lived in a world where wealth and family connections opened doors. He had no idea what it was like to be afraid. Or alone.

The driver hopped out and opened the door. "Here you are, Miss."

Surrounded by the spicy scent of leather, Miranda burrowed into the corner and let the tears fall. Hopefully the driver would concentrate on the traffic and not notice the woman falling apart in the backseat.

A cold numbness permeated every inch of her body until she felt as if she were encased in ice.

Was it possible Daniel's adoption hadn't been legal? It was something she'd always wondered. Lorraine, who'd shared everything with her, had been strangely reluctant to give Miranda details about Daniel's birth mother. At the time, she'd assumed Lorraine had wanted to concentrate on Daniel and not on the woman who'd put him up for adoption. In Lorraine's mind, Daniel had already belonged to her and she'd wanted to focus on the future, not the past.

Barnaby Harcourt had been a ruthless man who'd manipulated dozens of people during a traumatic time in their lives but Miranda repeatedly rejected the notion Lorraine and Tom had gotten mixed up in one of his schemes. Her sister had desperately wanted to be a mother but she wouldn't have done anything illegal to make her dream a reality.

But what if she and Tom hadn't known what Harcourt had been up to?

Miranda knew she should have left Chestnut Grove a long time ago. She'd stayed too long. Long enough for the people who frequented the diner to know she didn't volunteer information about her past. Long enough for the people she worked with to be curious about her.

Because they care about you.

Miranda pushed the thought away.

I care about you, Miranda.

Andrew's words pierced her soul. He believed she was capable of a crime. That she was no better than Barnaby Harcourt. He'd brought her flowers and invited her for dinner while knowing he was going to confront her about Daniel's adoption.

"Miss? Are you all right?" Miranda opened her eyes and saw the driver's reflection in the rearview mirror. "This is your house, right?"

Miranda managed to nod. Darcy wouldn't have Daniel back for at least another hour.

An hour to decide whether to stay or to go.

She held it together under the chauffeur's watchful eye but the minute she stumbled into her apartment, the tears came.

Impatiently, she brushed them away. She didn't have time to cry.

She had to come up with a plan.

Chapter Eighteen

The first thing Andrew did after Miranda walked out was make a phone call.

"I just talked to Miranda," Andrew told Ross without preamble. "Lorraine Ferris and Miranda were sisters. Miranda adopted Daniel after Lorraine and her husband died in a car accident. We need details about Daniel's birth mother to find out if Harcourt was blackmailing her. And we need to make sure Daniel's records weren't tampered with."

There was a long pause. "Ah… We?"

"Miranda left here pretty upset." An understatement. "She's afraid she could lose custody of Daniel and I'm going to do everything I can to make sure she doesn't."

Another pause. "Um, no offense, Andrew, but you aren't exactly experienced to handle this kind of situation."

Andrew smiled grimly. "That isn't exactly true."

"What do you mean?" Andrew could practically hear

the phrase *delusions of grandeur* bouncing around in Ross's head.

Andrew had encouraged Miranda to trust people and yet he hadn't been willing to do the same. He'd always told himself it was for their protection but maybe he'd felt better when he was in control of a situation. Not so different from Miranda. Maybe it was time to practice what he preached.

"Are you familiar with the Guardian?"

"I've heard the name. Everyone in law enforcement has. But I doubt he'll get involved. He specializes in finding missing children. I wouldn't even know how to find the guy. He's kept his identity a secret for years—"

"Yeah, I know. Probably living the life of the idle rich or something." Three, two, one…

Ross's sudden burst of laughter told Andrew the guy was quick. For a gumshoe.

"Okay, talk to me. What have you got in mind?"

"If you work on the adoption records, I'll call in some favors. Starting now."

"Starting now," Ross repeated the words wearily.

"Look at it as practice for those late-night strolls around the house with a fussy newborn."

"Thanks for the visual," Ross said wryly. "I'll put on a pot of coffee." Ross paused, choosing his next words carefully. "If Miranda is really Daniel's adoptive mother and everything was legal, why all the secrecy? What is she hiding?"

Andrew wondered the same thing but he wasn't ready yet to confide his suspicions to Ross. That Miranda wasn't hiding something—she was hiding *from* someone.

By tomorrow morning, he'd be able to write a book about Miranda Jones. And he planned to do everything he could to make sure she and Daniel got a happy ending.

Miranda was frightened enough to repack those suitcases and disappear into the night. He prayed that the changes he'd seen in her recently would be stronger than her fear.

By six o'clock in the morning, the only things keeping Andrew awake were the caffeine pumping through his blood and the growing list of details in the notebook at his elbow.

Miranda was thirty-four years old. And she'd never been married. That bit of information canceled out the bitter-divorce theory. She'd told Sandra the truth about working at a bank but had failed to mention graduating at the top of her class from the University of Georgia with a degree in finance.

A friend who worked for one of the major newspapers in Atlanta had searched the archives and confirmed the deaths of Lorraine and Tom Ferris on New Year's Eve. The accident had drawn major media coverage not only because the Ferrises were young parents, but because it involved a man whose license had been revoked due to three prior drunk-driving convictions. The obituary briefly mentioned survivors, including a son, Daniel, and a sister, Miranda, and noted the names of Lorraine's parents. Andrew read between the lines. The different last names and places of residence hinted the family wasn't close—physically or emotionally. If he had to guess, Daniel was the only real family Miranda had.

When the computer downloaded a photo of Lorraine and Tom, Andrew felt as if someone kicked him in the teeth. No one could doubt the two women were related. Lorraine's short, stylish haircut differed from Miranda's but they shared the same bone structure and winsome smile.

Miranda had lost so much. As he fit the pieces of her life together, a picture was forming of a young woman grieving the death of her only sibling while taking on the care and responsibility of an active toddler. Raising him as her own.

His respect for Miranda grew.

The phone chirped and Andrew swiped it up, hoping Ross had good news. "Hello?"

"You owe me, buddy," a voice rasped in his ear.

Tobias, a.k.a. "Toby" Rudley. A crusty ex-con who'd left the dark side to start a security business. Now he made a living hacking into corporate computers on a regular basis. Just to pinpoint the weak areas. So he said. Andrew had a hunch it was more for entertainment. Like watching HBO.

Andrew tapped his pen against the notebook. "I'll let you borrow my yacht for two weeks. What did you find out?"

"I worked with those dates you gave me and checked out the bank where she worked. Miranda Jones was promoted in January and fired in May."

Andrew frowned. Knowing Miranda's loyalty to Sandra and the diner, the promotion made sense. Getting fired didn't. "Why?"

"I'm getting there. Just for future reference, people

get cranky when you wake them up before they've had their first cup of coffee."

"Couldn't help it." Andrew tried to rein in his impatience. "Details, Tobe."

"Sorry. I tracked down a lady who worked with Miranda. According to her, Miranda dated a lawyer. She couldn't remember his name but thought he was a junior partner with one of the larger firms in the city. Anyway, the guy turned out to be a wacko with a capital *W*. Started dropping in at the bank a few times a day to check on Miranda. Called her a lot. One day he got a little hostile when Miranda's supervisor asked him to leave. Made a scene. That's when they fired her. Security escorted her out the door and no one saw her after that."

Andrew's breath hissed between his teeth. She *had* been hiding from someone. Not an ex-husband but a boyfriend. The fact he'd been right didn't make him feel better. "She had a stalker boyfriend and no one checked on her?"

"Whoa. Is this my fault? According to my source, no one really knew her. Your girl didn't socialize with the other employees."

Because she put Daniel first. As she did now.

"Did you find out the name of the lawyer?"

"How many weeks do I get the boat? Three?"

Andrew thought he'd mentioned two but he wasn't in the mood to negotiate. Long-term relationships with district attorneys had taught Toby how to deal. Andrew would *give* him the boat if it meant he got answers. "That's what I said."

"Yup. I have his name," Toby said cheerfully. "Hal Stevens. Resides at 404B Oceanview Terrace. Atlanta, Georgia. Never married. Quit the law firm a couple years back to start his own practice. He's padding his bank account defending nightclub owners now. The kind that get in trouble for adding an addendum to the job descriptions of the waitresses and dancers. You know what I'm saying?"

Toby always had an interesting way of describing things. So Stevens worked for the creatures sticking to the bottom of the food chain. It fit. What didn't make sense was why Miranda had fallen for a guy like that in the first place. The woman he knew and loved was smart and capable. But it might explain why she didn't trust herself when it came to men. He intended to prove to her she could trust *him.*

"You've been a big help, Toby." Andrew jotted the name Hal Stevens in the notebook.

"Does this mean you're going to stock the yacht with my favorite cigars?"

"You'll have to pound those nails in your own coffin, my friend. I want you around awhile."

"Aw, cut it out, Guardian, you're making me all weepy."

Andrew's lips twisted. "Take it easy on the coast guard this time. Your photo is still pinned to their bulletin board."

"They probably got it from the feds. Those guys have a scrapbook dedicated to me." Toby chuckled. "Just don't forget to invite me to the wedding. Miranda Jones is a looker. Not your usual type, though. Definitely the kind of girl you take home to meet Mama. The two of you made a cute couple."

Dread curled in his belly like the flick of a flame against paper. "What do you mean…we make a cute couple?"

"Fourth of July picnic…a picture of the two of you taken in a park in the quaint little burb you're living in. Ringing any bells?"

"Where did you see the photo?" Dread changed to fear in roughly the same amount of time it took his Porsche to go from zero to sixty.

"I saw it in some gossip rag at the gas station. Not that I make a habit of reading those things but I—"

"I'll talk to you later, Toby." Andrew flipped the phone shut and closed his eyes, sending up a plea for God to clean up a mess that might have just gotten messier. The photographer who'd snapped their picture at Winchester Park had been a freelancer for a tabloid with national distribution.

Great.

A relationship with Hal Stevens had put Miranda on the run. Best case scenario, the guy had had control issues. Worst case scenario, he'd been physically and emotionally abusive. But, in her love for Daniel, Miranda had found the courage and strength to break free.

I remember the scary place.

Daniel's soft-spoken words had wrung out Andrew's emotions and hung them up to dry.

He'd dealt with men like Stevens in the past. Obsessive. Controlling. They burned with the need to be in charge. To a guy like that, letting Miranda slip out of his grasp would equal failure. And failure wasn't acceptable.

Was Stevens still searching for her?

The suitcases and Miranda's reluctance to trust people told Andrew she believed he was. The barren apartment was a heart-wrenching testimony to Miranda's belief Hal would eventually catch up to her, forcing them to leave again. No wonder Miranda had resisted forming ties with Chestnut Grove and people like Sandra.

A verse filtered through Andrew's mind and settled in his heart.

He will cover you with his feathers, and under his wings you will find refuge; his faithfulness will be your shield and rampart.

The world had shrunk since the discovery of cyberspace. Finding people wasn't so difficult anymore. Andrew's heart missed a beat, struck by the truth. Only God's grace and mercy had kept Miranda and Daniel safely hidden over the past four years.

Please, God. Let Miranda realize it, too. Let her know You've always been there for her. That You haven't forgotten her.

Miranda watched the sun come up while Daniel slept in the next room. Now she found herself wishing she hadn't pulled down the drapes. She felt vulnerable. Exposed. Even though she'd turned the lights off and set her phone on mute.

Her churning thoughts matched the churning in her stomach. The suitcases waited in the closet. Empty. It would take fifteen minutes to fill them.

If they left.

What had prevented her from taking Daniel and leaving after Darcy had brought him home from the movie? The promise she'd made to Daniel that Chestnut Grove was home? Her blossoming friendship with Leah Cavanaugh? Her loyalty to Sandra and Isaac?

Andrew's plea to trust him?

She couldn't think about Andrew. She'd half expected him to follow her home. Or to call. But why would he? She'd told him she didn't want to have anything to do with him anymore. And he thought her capable of stealing a child....

"Mom?" Daniel's sleepy voice came from the doorway of his bedroom. "Are you taking me to Olivia's pretty soon?"

Miranda opened her arms and Daniel burrowed into them.

One more day wouldn't matter. If they left, she had to close out her savings account and give Mrs. Enderby notice. Sandra and Isaac had been good to her, so she couldn't just leave without a word. She'd have to say goodbye to Darcy...and thank Leah for offering to watch Daniel. All proof she'd stayed in Chestnut Grove too long. When she'd left Atlanta, pain hadn't shredded her heart. Not like now.

"Mom's not going to work today." Or maybe tomorrow, either.

"Why not?"

"I don't feel well," Miranda said in a husky voice, hoping Daniel wouldn't realize she'd been up all night. "But you can still play at Olivia's."

"Are you going to take a nap?" Daniel's voice thinned with worry and Miranda forced a smile.

"I think so. You get dressed and I'll make scrambled eggs."

"Okay." Daniel bounced off the couch and disappeared into the bedroom.

Miranda called the diner and left a message with Nina, one of the other waitresses, that she wouldn't be coming to work and scraped up enough energy to get off the couch and shuffle into the kitchen.

Mistake. The muted wild-rose walls reminded her of Sunday morning, when Andrew had shown up at the door with a paintbrush in his pocket.

The day he'd kissed her. The day she'd realized she was falling in love with him.

She couldn't separate the strands of pain that knotted her insides. Leaving Chestnut Grove. Daniel's adoption records being found. Andrew believing the worst of her. All of it made her steps as heavy as her heart.

She dropped Daniel off at the Cavanaughs' and saw Leah standing on the step with Joseph. Waiting for her. With a sinking heart, Miranda knew Leah planned to invite her to stay for coffee again. In the rearview mirror, she saw Leah's smile fade as she drove away.

The apartment was quiet when she let herself back in. She walked into Daniel's room and the tears started all over again. She scrubbed them away impatiently. She didn't have a choice.

She sat down on Daniel's bed and unearthed Lily from beneath the covers.

"I'm sorry, Daniel," she murmured as she unzipped the suitcase. Everything inside her rebelled against the task but she picked up Lily and put her inside.

Her fingers trailed over the soft leather of the baseball glove Andrew had given Daniel and then moved to the plaster handprint he'd made at Sonshine Camp. Her son, bless his organized little soul, had carefully propped up the card with the accompanying Bible verse next to it.

I have engraved you on the palms of my hands.

The words had been written so long ago, they couldn't be meant for her.

There was a time you believed they were.

That was before Lorraine and Tom had died. Before Hal…

What if Daniel was hurt? One of the conversations she'd had with Sandra echoed in her mind. *Wouldn't you want him to run to you if he was in pain?*

What if she took a step of faith and believed the promise? Would she experience the same kind of peace Sandra and Leah had? The kind that came from knowing no matter what happened, God was there?

Chapter Nineteen

"Bingo." Ross waved a piece of paper in the air. "This is what we've been looking for."

Andrew crossed the room in two strides. He'd decided to stop by Tiny Blessings to compare notes with Ross before going to see Miranda. He hadn't expected to find Eric Pellegrino, Pilar Fletcher and Kelly tirelessly working side by side with Ross, elbow deep in old files. Ross had filled them in on Miranda's situation and Andrew's fear that she'd leave town. Eric and Pilar had immediately rearranged their schedules to help out.

"What?" Twenty-four hours without sleep had roughened Andrew's voice but hadn't affected his determination.

"Daniel's original documents. We'll match them against the copies I found to see if Harcourt doctored them up."

Kelly and Pilar crowded in so close, their bellies bumped together. Pilar's giggle eased the tension in the room.

"Back up the bumper cars, ladies," Ross said, a hint of a smile playing at the corner of his mouth.

Andrew resisted the urge to snatch the paper from Ross's hand. He'd been going crazy wondering if Miranda had taken Daniel and left town. Maybe they'd found the reason to make her stay.

"I don't believe it." Ross slapped the papers down on the desk.

Andrew's heart stopped. "They're not the same."

"They're identical. That's what I can't believe," he corrected, a weary grin spreading across his face. "I have no idea why Harcourt stashed Daniel's records in the mansion but from what I can see here, these documents are legit. Daniel Thomas Jones's original adoption was perfectly legal."

Andrew stared down at the documents until Eric gave him a friendly shove to wake him up.

Kelly smiled and gave Andrew a knowing look. "Andrew, why don't you tell Miranda the good news? Ross is going home to take a nap."

"A nap—" Ross stifled a yawn "—sounds good."

Exhaustion had sucked the energy from Andrew's bones but sleep was the last thing on his mind. He picked up the documents.

"Can I borrow these?"

Ross nodded. "Be my guest."

Andrew had almost made it the door when Kelly's cell phone rang.

Darcy had grabbed Daniel's hand seconds after he and Miranda had walked into the diner.

"Hey, Miranda, do you mind if I take my favorite rug rat to the park for a while?"

Which meant Miranda looked as awful as she felt.

She didn't miss the look Darcy and Sandra exchanged, either. The words *tag team* came to mind but she forced a smile, grateful for the chance to talk to Sandra alone for a few minutes.

"Don't be gone too long. It's getting dark."

"Gotcha." Darcy grinned and herded Daniel out the door.

"She's not very subtle, is she?" Sandra smiled and untied her apron.

"No." Miranda watched them dash across the street, hand in hand. If she didn't get this over with, she'd lose her nerve completely.

Sandra pulled a chair away from the table and motioned for Miranda to sit down. "Are you feeling better? You look a little tattered around the edges, sugar."

Miranda choked back a laugh. "I feel a little tattered around the edges."

"Daniel's adoption records."

"You know?" Miranda stared at her, stunned, until she made the connection. Of course. Ross had found Daniel's records. He would have told Kelly, who would have confided in Sandra.

"Don't blame Kelly," Sandra said quickly, as if she'd read Miranda's mind. "Ross called me. He's concerned about you."

"And he told Andrew." Bitterness leaked into Miranda's voice.

"Only because I asked him to."

"You did?" That surprised her. "Why?"

"Because as much as I love Ross, he's a 'just the facts, ma'am' kind of guy. I was afraid if he told you Daniel's records were mixed in with the other ones Jonah'd found, you'd pack up and leave." Sandra reached out and squeezed her hand. "I thought Andrew could convince you to stay."

Miranda wound her fingers together. "He tried."

I can help you. There's something you don't know....

She'd cut him off, not willing to listen. In the end, it didn't matter. They had to leave. She'd struggled for hours and come to a conclusion late in the afternoon. She only hoped Daniel would understand.

But, first, she would tell Sandra. Her boss had been so good to them, she deserved to know.

"Chestnut Grove is your home. What's out there for you and Daniel?" Sandra asked softly.

Nothing. "I can't lose him, Sandra."

"Andrew and Ross are working to make sure that doesn't happen. You may not believe this, but people care about you. There are people who've been praying for you since the day you came to town. You might feel alone, but you aren't."

Miranda wanted to believe it. With all her heart she wanted to believe it.

"You've kept things locked up inside you for so long. It's time to let some light shine in. Then you'll see you don't have to carry all these burdens alone."

Sandra's compassionate words opened a floodgate. Stumbling over the harsh terrain of the past, Miranda told her about Lorraine and Tom and how she'd adopted

Daniel after their deaths. And about Hal and how attentive he'd been until his true colors had started to show. When the storm finally subsided, Miranda searched Sandra's eyes for signs of disgust or disapproval. All she saw was understanding. And love.

"God didn't make a mistake when He brought you to Chestnut Grove. He hasn't forgotten you." Tears filled Sandra's eyes. "Remember what I said about running? Go ahead and run. Right into His arms. That's where you're safe."

The thought filled Miranda with hope. She was tired of surviving instead of living. Tired of looking over her shoulder. She'd thought isolation meant protection but instead of a refuge, she'd created a prison. And she'd inadvertently put her son—the one she most wanted to protect—there, too. She loved Daniel too much to live like that anymore.

"I want to, Sandra…."

The door snapped open and Darcy rushed into the diner. Alone.

Miranda rose to her feet. "What's wrong?"

"Daniel's gone."

Andrew sped through two yellow lights on his way to the diner. Sandra met him at the door. Worry scored deep lines in her forehead and around her mouth. Her ready smile was absent, stirring the fear the unsettling phone call had created.

"Where's Miranda?"

"She's at the park. Darcy took Daniel over there to play while Miranda and I had a heart-to-heart. She came back a little while ago and said Daniel was gone. They'd been playing hide-and-seek—"

"Does Daniel know Miranda is thinking about leaving town?"

"I…I'm not sure." Sandra made the connection. "You think he ran away?"

Andrew had gotten in trouble before for making assumptions but he didn't believe Daniel would simply take off. He was the "man of the house." In some ways as protective of Miranda as she was of him.

The back door opened and Miranda came in, Darcy at her heels.

"Sandra, is he back—" Miranda froze when she saw Andrew.

It was now or never. He held out his hand. Miranda lurched forward and wove her fingers through his. Let him draw her against his side.

"We're going to find him," he promised, absorbing the tremor that racked her body.

"But it's been over an hour. And it's almost dark." Fear darkened her eyes.

"I called Zach at the PD, and officers are already responding. I'm going to take you home in case Daniel shows up there."

Miranda's chin lifted. "I have to go back to the park. I have to keep looking."

"Andrew's right, sweetheart." Sandra wrapped an arm around Darcy, who'd started to cry again. "And I'll wait right here until you call and tell me Daniel is home safe and sound."

Miranda sagged against Andrew for a moment but

when she looked up at him, the expression on her face blew him away. She had no idea who he was. The trust shimmering in her eyes was for Andrew Noble, not the Guardian. He didn't deserve it. He'd doubted her but it hadn't destroyed the fragile bond between them.

Thank you, God.

Zach Fletcher strode into the kitchen. He wore plain clothes but his off-duty weapon was clearly visible, tucked in a shoulder holster. "I've got officers combing the park but there's so sign of him yet. What's your plan?"

The fact that the Chestnut Grove detective had asked *him* meant Ross hadn't kept his secret. Not that it mattered at this point. What mattered was finding Daniel, but Andrew briefly wondered if Miranda had noticed Zach defer to him.

Andrew's cell phone hummed quietly in his pocket. "I've got to take this. I'll be back in a minute." He stepped into the dining room. "Ross? Go ahead."

"I just talked to some teenagers who saw a boy that fit Daniel's description. He was walking with a man near the pond about an hour ago."

Bile swirled in Andrew's stomach. "Did they give you a description of the guy?"

"About six feet tall. Blond hair. Between thirty and forty. That's all they could give me. They didn't pay much attention because Daniel didn't seem to be upset."

Knowing how protective Miranda was, she would have coached Daniel repeatedly about strangers. If the boy had gone with someone, chances were he knew him.

"Do you have access to a laptop?"

"In my car."

Van Zandt must have been a Boy Scout. Always prepared. Andrew would give him a hard time about it later. "I need a photo of Hal Stevens. My guess is he's had a few brushes with the law. His picture is in some police officer's wallet out there."

"Stevens. Got it."

The chances of Hal Stevens seeing the picture of Andrew and Miranda in the tabloid was slim but Andrew couldn't rule out the possibility. Hal was no fool. If he wanted to get to Miranda, all he had to do was get to Daniel first.

The thought of Daniel at the mercy of Stevens and the memory of his own abduction curdled his blood. Daniel would be counting on him. He knew it.

God, no matter where Daniel is, protect him. Show him that You're with him, just like You did for me. Help him stay strong. Help me find him....

With an *amen* still lingering on his lips, Andrew slipped back into the kitchen.

Miranda, Sandra and Darcy sat together at the table. Hands clasped. Heads bowed. But it wasn't Sandra leading the heartfelt prayer. It was Miranda.

Miranda felt an overwhelming sense of warmth and peace as she poured out her heart to God. Once she opened her heart, she felt His love and forgiveness wash away the weight of the past. What Sandra had said was true. God had been waiting for her to run to *Him.* And in His arms she felt whole. New.

"Are you ready to go?" Miranda's eyes flew open as Andrew's hands closed gently over her shoulders. She nodded, letting him draw her to her feet and lead her into the alley where his car was parked.

"Thank you for coming to the diner. And for helping." Her voice sounded stiff and formal, even to her own ears. She'd clung to Andrew like a vine when she'd seen him in the kitchen. It took another step of faith but she chose to believe Andrew wanted to help. She wasn't sure how he felt about her anymore, but she knew he cared about Daniel.

Andrew reached out in the darkness and his hand closed over hers, warm and strong. "I was on my way over here, anyway. I had something to tell you. Daniel's adoption was legal, Miranda. Do you hear me? It was legal. His records are clean. Lorraine and Tom didn't do anything wrong."

She tried to process the words. "Legal? But how can you be sure?" Logic battled against hope. "Lorraine wanted Daniel so much… She wouldn't tell me anything about his birth mother."

Andrew heard the tremor in her voice and knew Miranda must have struggled with that uncertainty for years. He could finally put her fears to rest.

"Daniel's birth mother, Rosalie Oliver, died a few hours after giving birth. She was sixteen years old when she found out she was pregnant but she'd already decided to keep her baby. Her parents had put Daniel up for adoption after she'd died. Maybe Lorraine had felt guilty knowing a loss in someone else's family had created hers."

Miranda thought about the tragedy that had brought Daniel into their lives and a lump formed in her throat.

"When Ross had found Daniel's family history, it looked like the type of situation Harcourt loved to take advantage of. But he hadn't. Probably because, even though Rosalie was a teenager, her parents had openly supported her instead of trying to hide it. He couldn't use it as blackmail."

Miranda tried to absorb everything he'd told her, but none of it mattered at the moment. Not when Daniel was missing.

"Where is he, Andrew?"

Andrew didn't answer her. He parked the car and went around to the other side. "Let's go inside."

Silently, they climbed the stairs to the apartment. Miranda's hands shook so badly Andrew took the key from her and opened the door.

And practically tripped over a suitcase.

"You decided to leave." Discouragement flattened his voice. When he'd walked into the kitchen and heard her praying, he'd hoped it meant she'd had a change of heart. The permanent kind.

"Yes," she admitted. "But then I went to see Sandra, hoping she'd talk me out of it."

Andrew walked over to the answering machine. The light glowed on the panel. No messages. If Stevens had Daniel, he'd be calling soon enough.

"What are you doing?" Miranda hurried over and stared down at the machine.

He exhaled. "Miranda, I know about Hal Stevens."

"Hal..." Miranda flinched. "How do you know about him?"

"I confronted you about not trusting people but I've

been guilty of the same thing. You've been protecting Daniel and I've been protecting my work." He led her to the couch and drew her down beside him. "When I was five years old, a family employee abducted me and held me for ransom for four days. The only thing that kept me from going crazy was telling myself stories from the children's Bible my grandmother had given to me. I couldn't read yet, but I remembered the pictures. Especially the one of Daniel in a pit, surrounded by lions. It's when God became real to me."

Miranda's silence encouraged him to continue. "After I graduated from college, I got discouraged hearing story after story about missing children—I knew firsthand what they were going through. I felt God nudging me to do something to help." Andrew smiled a little wryly. "Enter a very large trust fund and a family name that got people's attention. From there, I developed a network of people and funded the resources necessary to locate missing children. The first boy I'd found gave me a nickname. Guardian. The people who need to get hold of me know how to, but if the press got wind of it, the whole thing might crash. The publicity might handicap what I do. I never wanted to take the risk." He had to tread carefully now. "When I used those connections to search for information about you and Daniel last night, I found out about Hal."

Miranda stiffened.

"It took a lot of courage to leave Atlanta." His thumb brushed the side of her face and absorbed the tears tracking her cheek. "But it's possible Hal knows you're here now."

"How?" Her anguished cry cut through him like cold steel.

"A picture of us taken together at the Fourth of July picnic ended up in a tabloid. He might have seen it."

Miranda rose to her feet and wrapped her arms around her middle. "You'll find him, won't you?"

"I will." He drew her into his arms and rested his head against hers for a brief moment. "I should have brought Darcy along. I don't want to leave you alone."

Miranda's lips trembled but she managed a smile. "I'm not alone."

Chapter Twenty

Miranda watched Andrew's car disappear down the street.

Fear threatened to engulf her again and, for the first time, she asked God to take it away.

I trust You, Lord. I know Daniel is safe in Your care. And thank You for keeping Andrew safe all those years ago.

She shivered when she thought of Andrew as a child, frightened and alone. At the mercy of a stranger. It could have crippled him emotionally for the rest of his life but instead he had let God use it to begin a personal crusade. He'd let people dismiss him as carefree and irresponsible, and deliberately encouraged the media to play up the image so he'd be free to pursue his work as the Guardian.

She'd caught glimpses of those hidden depths in him but fear and mistrust had kept her at a distance. Again. She'd been protecting her heart, not realizing he'd stolen it that moment in the diner when he'd winked at Daniel, his shoes covered in syrup and egg yolks.

Maybe it was time to stop running from her emotions, too. But would Andrew believe her? She'd rejected his help. Told him she didn't want to see him again.

Someone tapped quietly on the door and she flew over to it, praying Daniel would be there. Instead, Ross Van Zandt stood on the other side.

"Did you find him?"

"Not yet." Ross clearly wished he had different news to report. "Andrew asked me to drop by and give you this. He said it might help."

Miranda took the brown package from him. "Thank you."

Ross raked his hand through his hair. "If anyone can find Daniel, Andrew can." His lips tilted slightly. "Who would've thunk it?" he murmured.

I would.

Miranda didn't say the words out loud but they bloomed in her heart. She couldn't believe she'd ever compared him to Hal. The two men were nothing alike. Andrew had accepted her—fears and all—and seen something valuable in her. Instead of chiding her for getting involved with Hal, he'd praised her courage for leaving him.

"I've got to check back in. We're praying for you and Daniel," Ross said. "We'll find him, Miranda. I promise. The Guardian—Andrew—he's good at what he does."

He disappeared down the stairs and Miranda reached into the bag and pulled out a thick, well-worn book. A children's Bible. The one that had comforted Andrew when he'd been abducted. She curled up in the chair by the window and paged through it until she found the story of Daniel.

There he was. Cowering in the corner of a dark pit, surrounded by lions. On the next page, they slept peacefully beside him. Daniel slept, too. With a smile on his face. A radiant light bathed the interior of the pit.

The door to her apartment opened unexpectedly and Kelly, Pilar, Anne, Meg and Leah tumbled in.

"I understand you need to be here in case Daniel comes home but I couldn't believe it when Ross told me they'd left you here alone," Kelly said, rolling her eyes.

"We'll stay as long as you need us, honey." Anne, Leah and Meg gathered her in for a group hug. The warmth of their presence thawed away some of the icy numbness that had invaded her limbs.

"I'll put on a pot of coffee," Pilar said.

Kelly wrapped a crocheted throw around Miranda's shoulders and pushed her gently toward the couch.

"Have you eaten anything, Miranda?" Anne wanted to know.

Miranda thought for a minute. Actually, she hadn't eaten anything all day. But the thought of food turned her stomach.

Anne clucked her tongue. "That's what I thought. I'll make an omelet."

"I don't think I—"

Kelly squeezed her hand. "You've got two pregnant women and a nursing mom in your house. We'll help you eat it."

Miranda quietly thanked God for the caring women who'd gathered in her tiny living room. She didn't belong in the circle of their friendship, yet, they'd rallied around her. It was a blessing she hadn't expected.

The telephone rang, piercing the quiet of the apartment.

Heart pounding, Miranda hurried to answer it. Andrew had told her he'd call her with any news.

"Hello?"

"Well, well. Miranda Jones." The smooth whisper of a voice came straight out of her worst dreams. "It's been a long time."

"Hal? Where is Daniel? Is he all right?"

"That's all you've got to say? Haven't you missed me?"

Miranda's knees went weak and she grabbed the back of the chair for support. "Let me talk to him."

"I warned you all I had to do was find the kid and I'd find you. Remember, Miranda?"

Like the gruesome details of a nightmare. "What do you want, Hal?"

"I want you," he said with chilling matter-of-factness. "You're going to come back to Atlanta with me. You and Danny. It's where you belong."

"Daniel and I belong here." Miranda licked her lips. "Please…let me talk to him."

"I might let you talk to him. Later. But first you have to talk to me." Hal chuckled, relishing the opportunity to be in control. "You weren't faithful, Miranda. I saw the picture of you and Noble. To be honest, I'm disappointed."

The line went dead.

"Hal?" Miranda shrieked his name into the phone, knowing he deliberately broke the connection to torment her. Helplessly, she turned to the women clustered around her. "He wouldn't tell me where they are."

"It doesn't matter." Kelly smiled faintly. "Now Andrew and Ross know."

The young police officer who appeared at the door less than fifteen minutes later to bring Miranda to the police department couldn't offer many details, but the one he did was all Miranda needed to hear.

They'd found Daniel.

The ride to the department seemed to take forever. The squad car had barely come to a complete stop and Miranda opened the door and leaped out.

Zach met Miranda and the officer in the lobby of the PD, his expression grim. "Miranda. Will you come with me, please? We need to ask you some questions."

Fear skittered through her as she followed him into the interview room. And came face-to-face with Hal.

Lines of dissipation marred the face she'd once thought handsome and his smile held only a fraction of the charm she remembered. He reached out to her and Miranda instinctively recoiled. Zach tensed and stepped between them.

"Miranda." Hal glanced at Zach and hesitated. Then he raised his hands and smiled beseechingly at Miranda. "Can you clear this up, sweetheart? I've been trying to convince your friends in blue that I had your permission to take Daniel for the evening."

Sickened, Miranda met his gaze. The husky timbre of his voice pleaded with her to set things right but there was no mistaking the threat in those pale blue eyes.

"I..." Miranda's mouth dried up.

"Mr. Stevens claims he's an old friend of yours," Zach said evenly. "And that you planned to meet tonight after the diner closed."

"That's right." Hal shot the detective a wounded look to generate some guilt for the way he'd been mistreated. "Tell him, Miranda."

Fear gripped Miranda's heart. If she lied to Zach, they'd let Hal go and he'd force her to go back to Atlanta with him. If she told the truth, she still wouldn't be free of him. Hal would be convicted of kidnapping and serve some time but he'd know right where to find her and Daniel again. They'd never be safe.

Yes, you will. Remember where you are, Miranda. You're in the palm of My hand.

The words swept through her like a warm breeze, clearing her mind and warming her heart. She was through running. No matter how afraid she was, she chose to believe the promise.

"He's lying, Detective Fletcher. I didn't give him permission to take Daniel."

Disbelief darkened Hal's eyes and then he lunged toward her. "You—"

Before Miranda could blink, the young patrol officer had Hal pressed against the wall and in handcuffs.

"Read Mr. Stevens his rights and find a comfortable place for him to spend the night," Zach barked. He looked down at Miranda and offered her his arm.

"Come with me, Miss Jones. I know someone who's very anxious to see you."

Andrew heard the click of the door and drew in a ragged breath when it opened and he saw Miranda standing there. She looked as if she were fresh off the battlefield—and maybe in a sense she was—but a warm light coaxed out the gold in her eyes and she managed a wan smile.

He'd known his lady would come through.

He'd been praying for her ever since Zach had escorted an apologetic there's-been-a-mistake-officer Hal Stevens to the department.

The guy was a piece of work. Minutes after they'd gotten a lock on his position and had burst into the hotel room, he'd played his part to the hilt. Feigning confusion, he'd immediately cooperated with Zach, explaining Miranda had invited him to Chestnut Grove for a visit. When he'd seen Daniel in the park, he'd claimed Daniel had told him Miranda wouldn't mind if they hung out together until they met later in the evening for their "date."

If Andrew hadn't already known the real situation, one look at the terror etched in Daniel's face had told him the boy had probably been threatened within an inch of his life if his story contradicted his abductor's. Daniel had skirted around Hal and barreled into Andrew's arms, whispering four words that had almost wrecked him.

I knew you'd come.

Andrew wanted to pound Stevens into the ground but

decided to let the feds do that in their own special way. Toby had managed to finagle another week on the yacht by calling with some new information. Andrew figured kidnapping added to fraud and tax evasion would put Stevens away for a long time.

As soon as they'd hustled Stevens into a squad car, Zach had taken over. The way things usually worked, Andrew stepped away from the situation and went home.

Not this time.

Daniel had clung to him like a monkey all the way to the police department and Andrew hadn't been in a hurry to let him go. He knew Zach had to question Miranda and get her side of the story. He'd prayed God would give her the strength to stand against Hal.

The expression on Miranda's face told Andrew He had.

"Mom!" Daniel flew into her arms and Miranda burst into tears. "It's okay." Awkwardly, he patted her back. "I knew Andrew would find me."

Through blurry eyes, Miranda watched Andrew break away from the wall and saunter toward them. Choking back another sob, she let him draw both her and Daniel into the comfort of his arms.

"Thank you," she murmured. It didn't feel like enough. Not after all he'd done for them.

"How do you feel about going home?" he said, and hiked Daniel onto his shoulder. "This guy's just about done in."

So was she.

The car ride was quiet. Andrew drove while Miranda

sat in the backseat, her arms around Daniel as he dozed against her.

As they neared the diner, Miranda noticed all the lights still on inside.

Andrew pulled the car along the curb. "Let's stop for a minute."

He got out first and eased Daniel out of Miranda's arms.

"What's going on?" Miranda climbed out, blinking in surprise at the number of people she could see gathered in the dining room.

"I'll let Sandra explain." Andrew smiled and opened the door. The enthusiastic cheer that greeted their arrival woke up Daniel and he lifted his head off Andrew's shoulder, blinking sleepily at the faces around him.

Kelly pulled Miranda into the room, laughing at the dazed expression on her face.

"Sandra called Naomi Fraser," she explained. "Apparently the Chestnut Grove Community Church prayer chain decided to meet at the diner tonight."

Miranda balked. "To pray for *Daniel?*"

"You're family, Miranda," Leah said, and gave Miranda's arm a gentle squeeze.

Anne winked. "She's right. You better get used to it."

Miranda shyly scanned the smiling faces of the people gathered around the tables. "I think I will."

Reverend Fraser ruffled Daniel's hair. The boy smiled in return and suddenly they were surrounded by the people who'd spent the evening fervently praying for his safe return.

Sandra kissed Miranda's cheek. "You take the day

off tomorrow, sugar. You deserve it." She lowered her voice. "You can spend the time unpacking those suitcases of yours."

Miranda smiled. "I didn't get very far," she admitted.

"That's good, because you're right where you are supposed to be." Sandra turned to the prayer warriors gathered in the diner. "Pie and coffee on the house for everyone. We're celebrating."

"Ready to go?" Andrew pressed his hand against her back and the warm contact sent little jolts of electricity dancing through her.

She nodded, suddenly unable to speak.

By the time they reached her apartment, Daniel had fallen asleep against her shoulder, his breathing even and untroubled.

Andrew carried him upstairs to the apartment and laid Daniel on the bed, carefully pulling off his shoes. Miranda relived that fleeting fanciful moment when she'd wondered what it would be like to be a family. To be the one Andrew didn't leave. The one he loved.

"Andrew?" Daniel sat up groggily.

"What is it, champ?" Andrew sat on the edge of the bed.

"Are you gonna leave?" The uncertainty in Daniel's voice tugged at Miranda's heart.

The shadows hid Andrew's expression but he nodded. "I'm going home to get some sleep. But how about I pick you and your mom up in the morning and we go to the beach?"

Daniel grinned. "All right."

Miranda walked out of the room and caught a glimpse of her reflection in the mirror on the wall.

She looked terrible. Purple smudges under her eyes. Her hair loose and wild. Rumpled T-shirt and jeans faded with age.

It was crazy to think Andrew was interested in anything more than friendship. Guardian or not, he'd end up with a woman comfortable in his world. Someone stylish and classy…

His reflection joined hers in the mirror. Two days of stubble shadowed his jaw and lines of fatigue bracketed his mouth.

He took her breath away. And so did the words he murmured in her ear.

"I love you, Miranda Jones."

She closed her eyes. When she opened them, he hadn't disappeared.

She gulped and stumbled blindly into the living room. He caught up to her.

"Running away again?"

"No." She smiled and his love gave her the courage to step boldly into his arms. "Sandra was right. I'm right where I'm supposed to be."

His arms tightened around her and when he smiled, Miranda saw the future in his eyes. And it was full of promise.

"I love you, too…" The words got lost in his kiss.

When they finally moved apart, Andrew looked as dazed as she felt.

"Marry me," he whispered. "I won't rush you into anything but I want the three of us to be together. To be a family. When you're ready—"

"I'm ready!" Daniel bounced out of the bedroom,

wide-awake, and bounded over to them. "How about tomorrow?"

"*Daniel.*" A breathless laugh escaped. "Tomorrow is...too soon." Her two favorite men stared at her in disappointment. She glanced at Andrew. "Isn't it?"

"I don't know." Andrew shrugged, a wicked twinkle in his eyes. "I do have...connections. I might be able to arrange it."

He was teasing her but Miranda loved it. "How?"

"You'll just have to trust me."

Miranda moved back into the shelter of his arms and smiled up at him.

"I do."

* * * * *

Dear Reader,

It was so much fun to revisit the characters in Chestnut Grove (and get to know new ones) in this continuation of the A TINY BLESSINGS TALE series.

As Miranda and Andrew's story came to life, I was reminded of how tempting it is to want people to heal on our timetable. Past hurts in Miranda's life made her wary of accepting friendship and trusting others, but the believers in Chestnut Grove didn't give up on her. God's faithfulness was reflected in their loving patience, until Miranda eventually made the decision to trust Him, too!

I hope you continue reading A TINY BLESSINGS TALE. There are more exciting stories as the series continues!

Please visit me at www.loveinspiredauthors.com or www.SteepleHill.com. I'd love to hear from you.

In Him,

Kathryn Springer

QUESTIONS FOR DISCUSSION

1. Andrew didn't get upset when people misjudged him, because he knew working undercover as "the Guardian" was God's will for his life. Have you ever been misjudged by others based on choices you've made? How? How did it make you feel?

2. What were Miranda's strengths and weaknesses? What did you most admire about her character?

3. Sandra Lange never gave up on Miranda. She prayed for her and loved her even when Miranda was afraid to form friendships. Ultimately, Sandra was the one Miranda turned to at a crucial point in her life. Has God ever put a "Miranda" in your life? Someone in your area of influence that you refused to give up on? Who is it?

4. Meg, Anne, Pilar and Rachel met at the Starlight Diner every Sunday for brunch. Do you have a group of "lifetime" friends you meet with on a regular basis? What are the needs these deep friendships meet in the lives of women?

5. What do you think first attracted Andrew to Miranda? At what point did Miranda begin to see there is more to Andrew than what the newspapers said?

6. What is the significance of the unpacked suitcases in Miranda's closet? Why do you think she never replaced the clothing as Daniel grew?
7. Miranda realized she'd never created a real home for Daniel. Instead of wallowing in guilt, she determined to start fresh by decorating the apartment. What were the changes she made? What did those changes reflect?
8. Both Andrew and Miranda had trust issues. In what ways were they alike? How were they different?
9. Is there a Bible story you read as a child that had a significant impact on your faith as an adult? Which one?
10. What was your favorite scene in the book? Why?

TITLES AVAILABLE NEXT MONTH

Don't miss these four stories in August

IN HIS DREAMS by Gail Gaymer Martin
Escape to beautiful Beaver Island could be the answer to Marsha Sullivan's problems. Since her husband's death, Marsha had lost her way, but being with her widowed brother-in-law Jeff and his daughter made her feel like part of a family once again.

MISSIONARY DADDY by Linda Goodnight
A Tiny Blessings Tale

Samantha Harcourt never forgot the handsome missionary she met abroad, but she never expected to see him in Chestnut Grove. He was trying to find homes for the world's orphans, including two he's crazy about. Could Samantha help Eric Pellegrino make a loving home for the four of them?

THE COLOR OF COURAGE by Patricia Davids
Only faith sustained Lindsey Mandel after the loss of her beloved twin brother. Now a freak accident would test the U.S. Army corporal's mettle once again. Desperate to save her brother's injured horse, Lindsey would have to put her trust in handsome veterinarian Brian Cutter.

TRUSTING HIM by Brenda Minton
Since the day he left prison, Michael Carson sought a second chance. Working alongside youth leader Maggie Simmons seemed like the perfect plan. Michael prayed he could resist old temptations and keep God—and Maggie—close to his heart.

LICNM0707